T0129338

The
Babbling
Brook

Gino Bumeliani

THE BABBLING BROOK

iUniverse books may be ordered through booksellers or by contacting:

iUniverse
1663 Liberty Drive
Bloomington, IN 47403
www.iuniverse.com
1-800-Authors (1-800-288-4677)

ISBN: 978-1-5320-5213-2 (sc)
ISBN: 978-1-5320-5212-5 (e)

Library of Congress Control Number: 2018908427

Print information available on the last page.

iUniverse rev. date: 07/24/2018

PROLOGUE

THIS IS A STORY OF TWO FAMILIES AND their love of the outdoors who meet in the hills of Halliburton when the Henderson's buy an old abandoned cabin. Their neighbours would be the Banks and as they get to know each other, the relationship that the families build together is legendary. As their children meet and grow together the two oldest children find friendship, respect and unbridled love. This love would be tested in the future. True love always wins out. The love found within the pages of this book is the kind of love that we should be so lucky to find.

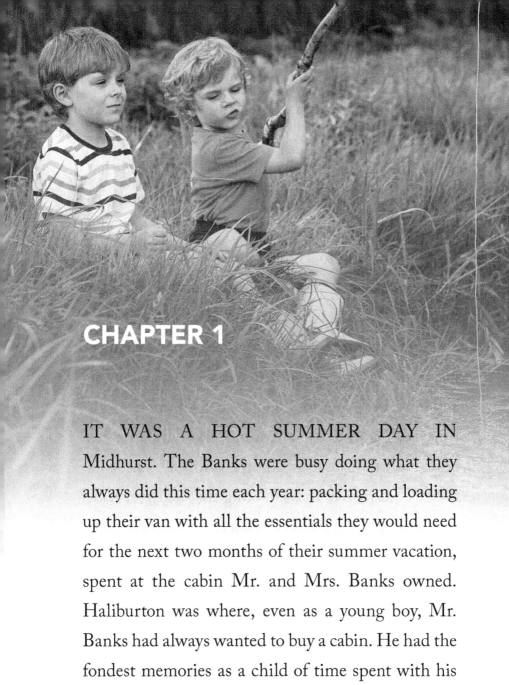

CHAPTER 1

IT WAS A HOT SUMMER DAY IN Midhurst. The Banks were busy doing what they always did this time each year: packing and loading up their van with all the essentials they would need for the next two months of their summer vacation, spent at the cabin Mr. and Mrs. Banks owned. Haliburton was where, even as a young boy, Mr. Banks had always wanted to buy a cabin. He had the fondest memories as a child of time spent with his father, whom he adored, fishing in the brooks and streams that were in an abundance.

In Midhurst, he would recall the nights before they would go fishing because, with all his excitement, he could not find a way to fall asleep and would always be so tired the next morning. He remembered that he would fall asleep on the two-hour journey to Haliburton. It was his dream that one day, he could bring his family to Haliburton, so he pursued his dream by opening his own business as the owner of Bank's Pools and Hot Tubs. He was so proud and often referred to himself as a high school part-timer. He would always tell anyone who would listen, he had done very well for a guy who spent most of his time fishing and not attending class. But not his boys. He would do everything possible to make sure they would receive the schooling that he never had.

Although Mr. Banks couldn't be prouder of how his personal life had been, he felt that, unlike his dad, he would spend as much time as he could with his family. He wanted to not only spend the occasional weekend fishing, but the whole summer with his family as well. He worked his butt off and he did everything to make sure that he was successful. He had a dotting wife. Her name was Elizabeth and two wonderful sons that he adored in every way.

Preston was the eldest and then there was his lively and mischievous son Drew.

Mr. Banks would always live in the shadow of his father-in-law Mr. Alexander Smith, because when he asked for his wife's hand in marriage, Mr. Smith who was an aristocrat, would not approve of the marriage of Elizabeth Smith to pool salesman Harry Banks, but Mr. Banks would prevail because Elizabeth could not bear her life without him. In those days Harry was tall, muscular and very good looking, with a full head of hair, unlike today. Although today, Mr. Banks is a successful businessman, who owned six locations in Midhurst. His greatest joy these days was sticking it to his father-in-law.

Putting all his feelings aside, the best thing business success brought was the fact that he and his family could spend two months together in the woods in their cabin in the beautiful region of Haliburton. He felt that he had gained success despite his father in-law, but this was not the only thing that made him want to be successful. He wanted to give his children the knowledge that one day, when they too were fathers, they would know he had shown his sons that family was the single most important accomplishment.

CHAPTER 2

MEANWHILE, IN THE TOWN OF Springwater, there was another family called the Henderson's. Chris Henderson and his wife Mary had a beautiful young daughter named Annabelle. Although Mr. Henderson had a much different upbringing with his family life, he knew that he would make his own family's life much better. He was a man who would never try to "keep up with the Jones". He wanted his family to enjoy life every day and wasn't going to wait until he was to old to fully achieve his goal. Mr. Henderson had worked for many years as a top-notch car salesman and after a few years opened his own dealership, simply named Henderson's Fine Cars.

After a couple of years of successful business, Mr. Henderson came across a cabin that had come on the open market in beautiful country of Haliburton. Without letting Mary and Annabelle know he had purchased the cabin which, as it turned out, was located next door to the Banks. When Chris got home that first night, after receiving the news that he had been the successful bidder for the cabin, he could barely contain his excitement, finally letting his family know that they were the new proud owners of a summer getaway in Haliburton.

That night sitting around the table having dinner with his two beautiful women and grinning from ear to, ear, Chris dropped the keys and the deed to their new cabin onto the table. Imagine Chris's satisfaction, watching his daughter Annabelle jump to her feet with excitement, Mary asking Annabelle to settle down and hearing the tiny scream of surprise let out by both the women. Anabelle herself was almost leaping out of her shoes with excitement and asking her father if they could go now. Chris simply looked at his daughter and said "Friday." Mary had tears in her eyes. She could not have been more proud of her husband's success and the pure joy on his face at being able to provide such a wonderful life for his two girls.

CHAPTER 3

ANOTHER SUMMER AND HALIBURTON here we come! It was early Friday morning and the Banks' boys had been up since 2 am, with excitement of the prospect of a wonderful summer in Haliburton. The boys had gone into their parent's room, had woken them up from a deep sleep and of course Mrs. Banks was enthralled with her boys' excitement. Mr. Banks not so much. He told the boys to relax, the van was already packed, and we would go as soon as daddy and mommy got ready. But Drew, being Drew, was like a hummingbird in his mother and father's ears, so Mrs. Banks went downstairs and made breakfast for the family as Mr. Banks got himself ready. The boys scarfed down their breakfast, making sure their parents finished just as fast. When Mrs. Banks was done tidying up, Mr. Banks made sure the house was secure and made sure everyone was in the van ready to go. Of course, the boys were ready, they had been ready since they woke up. Mr. Banks, got in the car, adjusted the mirrors and looked at Mrs. Banks and the boys and said "now, we are ready to go" and they were off.

As usual every time they went somewhere, the boys would ask every few minutes "are we there yet?" Mr. Banks would have a snared grin on his face. "Boys settle down. We are only a few minutes from the cabin." And, sure enough, as they approached the cabin, Mrs. banks just knew her boys would love their time there and how much it made Mr. Banks happy to be able to bring them to Haliburton. It made her feel so warm inside and proud of her husband.

When they had come to a complete stop, the boys made a B-line straight for the babbling brook and as boys will do, they would push and shove each other all the way there. Mr. and Mrs. Banks simply smiled at each other and knew they were home. The Banks' unloaded the vehicle as their children played. Mrs. Banks said to Mr. Banks, "Harry have you realized that the old Murphy place has a "sold" sign on it?" Mr. Banks replied "it took a while, but I guess we will have new neighbours." Mrs. Banks replied, "I hope they are friendly. It would be nice if they had small children because the Murphy's were very grumpy." Mr. Banks said "well, I guess we will find out soon enough." For most of the morning, the boys had been swimming in the brook as they always did, laughing and giggling as if life could not be any better.

When the boys were very little, Mr. Banks had built a treehouse in the sprawling old oak tree that was set back a couple hundred feet on the property. Mr. Banks had spared no expense so they had a Zip line, and it was completely furnished to the 9's for their boys to play in. He gave his boys everything he wished he had. He knew that his father would have loved to have given him the same, but Mr. Banks father could never afford the luxuries in life that his family enjoys today. Elizabeth looked over at her husband and saw he was day dreaming. She told Mr. Banks to get the boys as lunch was on the table.

The boys asked their father "if they could stay out a little longer and play" and Mr. Banks, replied, "it's our first day, we have two months left." The boys where huffing and puffing at that point. Mr. Banks looked back, noticed that his wife wasn't watching, so he ran up into the tree house and played the tickle game with his boys until he heard his wife calling once again. He looked at his boys and then told them "let's not keep your mother waiting."

And with that the three of them ran back to the cabin and started their lunch. When lunch was done, the boys asked their mother if they could go for a nap and knowing that the boys had had a long day, starting with their early morning trip, the boys went for their nap while Mr. and Mrs. Banks tidied up.

While Mr. Banks sat at the table with a beer, Mrs. Banks was washing the dishes and looking out her window. She spotted the new neighbours driving down their path. She was trying not to make it look so obvious that she checking out who was going to moving in after so many years. The Murphy's were what you might call unpleasant neighbours and she had always been on pins and needles when the children were playing outdoors, worrying they would go on the Murphy's land. Still, she wasn't going to let the new families see her spying but when the Henderson's came to a stop she saw Mr. & Mrs. Henderson and Anabelle get out of the vehicle. Elizabeth said to Harry "our new neighbours are here and they have a small daughter probably the same age as Preston. "Harry simply asked "how to do they look to you?" "Like sticks in the mud?" and Elizabeth replied "oh Harry let's keep an open mind." She told Harry that it would be nice if they welcomed their new neighbours with a pie and Harry obliged laughingly saying "I will get double everything, so you can make me a pie too," so Elizabeth wrote a list of ingredients for Harry to take to the corner store. She had decided to make her famous blueberry crumble pie putting the kind of smile on Harry's face that only food or money could bring.

Harry went to the corner store and gathered all the ingredients but after Harry was done, he noticed some of his friends going to the local pub and decided to share in a few himself. After a few pints Harry decided to get himself home because he knew that Elizabeth would be waiting. When Harry walked through the door, Mrs. Banks had asked him "where have you been, I've been waiting for two hours?". Mr. Banks said he stopped in for a few pints with his friends and although Mrs. Banks was unimpressed, she grabbed the bags of ingredients from her husband with a wry smile.

The boys were sleeping and they both arose to the smell of mom's favourite blueberry crumble pie. They both jumped up to their feet and quickly scurried downstairs where, to their amazement, mom had baked two of her famous pies. Drew ran to the kitchen cupboard, grabbed a spoon, ready to dive in at that point when Mrs. Banks came back into the kitchen and said to Drew "Stop right their young man!" "Those pies are for our new neighbours!"

Preston was a quiet and reserved boy and did not say a word. He understood, but Drew on the other hand, protested until his mother told him that was enough. The boys were both loving sons who were very close to each other but Preston, being the oldest, was the leader and most of the time Preston would cover for his younger brother when they would find themselves in deep water. It wasn't like Mrs. Banks wasn't aware of this brotherly bond but that's why Preston was always "her little sweet heart" and Drew was "her little devil" but she loved them both equally. Drew asked his mom if he could go outside and play and Preston, in his shy voice, asked "do we have new neighbours' mom?" Mrs. Banks looked in her boy's eyes and said "yes and they have a little girl." Mrs. Banks could see that her handsome son Preston had a sheepish grin and a rushing face of blush and smiled to herself realizing she had made her son uncomfortable. She looked at Preston and said "so go play outside with Drew and keep him out of trouble." Preston obliged while Mrs. Banks joined her huband on the sofa for a little rest and relaxation.

CHAPTER 4

AS THE HENDERSON'S GOT SETTLED IN their new summer cabin, Annabelle looked at her parents and said "I can't believe how lucky I am." Mr. and Mrs. Henderson both smiled. Annabelle remarked to her parents "life will never be the same again." Mary had set a late lunch at the table and once lunch was done and everything had been put away, Annabelle said to her parents "come on mom and dad I want to explore Haliburton." Mary said "we have the whole summer, honey. We don't have to do it all in one day." So, the Henderson's set out and started exploring all the surroundings that

Haliburton and their new summer home had to offer them. They found many streams and a few lakes, and birds in their natural habitat.

Although they had enjoyed all there was to see, out of the corner of her eye, Annabelle had noticed a boy sitting on a rock, reading a book. She thought he was a cute boy but she thought it was weird that he read his book sitting alone on a rock by the babbling stream. It seemed like he was in a daze and she wondered why was he just seating there? He wasn't like any boy that she had seen, so lost in his book. She had figured that he wasn't much older than her and wanted to go over and sit by him and introduce herself, but she stood there for a while and watched this interesting boy. Her father had noticed and yelled at Annabelle "come on dear we still have much to see."

Annabelle said "I'm coming father." They enjoyed the rest of the afternoon walking around stopping to smell all the odours in their new surroundings. The Henderson's couldn't be more proud of their young daughter and as they discovered the true beauty of this majestic place, that they now owned a summer home. Chris looked at his wife and his child and knew that he had given them a place that he hoped would make many happy memories. He asked the women that shared his wonderful happy life, for a family hug. They laid out a blanket and sat by the brook enjoying the sounds and views of this beautiful land and before they knew it, it was getting dark, so they started their trek back home.

Once the Hendersons arrived back home, Mrs. Henderson asked Annabelle to go wash up and although Annabelle herself felt that she had not got messy in any way went to wash up without a word of protest. Mr. and Mrs. Henderson proceeded to cook their first dinner in their new summer home. Chris looked at Mary and said "I think it's time to celebrate" and opened a bottle of champagne to celebrate all the success that they have achieved together, both agreeing that Annabelle was their greatest happiness.

Mrs. Henderson had made Annabelle's favourite meal, which was spaghetti and meatballs. As they were completing dinner, Annabelle said to her parents that "this was the best day of her life." She could hardly wait for every other day to come. Once again Mr. Henderson looked at his adoring young girl and although he knew that money doesn't make happiness, in this case it was exactly what his hard work did. It was the way to give his family something that, as a child, he thought was only possible in books and movies and he felt so warm inside. He knew that this was where they were meant to be.

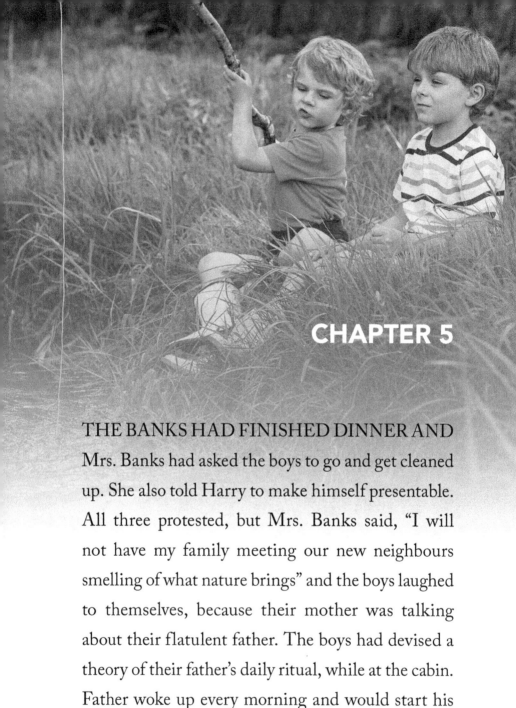

CHAPTER 5

THE BANKS HAD FINISHED DINNER AND Mrs. Banks had asked the boys to go and get cleaned up. She also told Harry to make himself presentable. All three protested, but Mrs. Banks said, "I will not have my family meeting our new neighbours smelling of what nature brings" and the boys laughed to themselves, because their mother was talking about their flatulent father. The boys had devised a theory of their father's daily ritual, while at the cabin. Father woke up every morning and would start his day fishing, coming back to the cabin, having a big lunch and then make his usual visit to the potty. The boys knew, however, that it was better to keep their thoughts between themselves, not for their mother or father to hear.

Although the boys protested, they did what their mother said, including Harry. When the boys were finished, they came bounding down the stairs. Mrs. Banks shook her head because the boy's shirts were hanging out of their pants and Harry's as well. She often wondered where the handsome man that was always dressed to the nines in younger years had gone to. She had a good laugh to herself, as a loving wife and mother her role would always be to make sure their appearance was neat and tidy. Mrs. Banks told all three of them to be on their best behaviour. She picked up her magnificent pie and marched over to welcome the new neighbours.

The Henderson's were wrapping up their dinner when they suddenly heard a knock on their door. Mr. Henderson looked at his wife Mary, and said "are you expecting anyone dear?" She said "no" but are you going to sit there or do you think the door is going to open on its own?" "No. Well then answer the door." When Mr. Henderson opened the door, it was the Banks standing there, pie in hand. Mary, with her upbringing, simply welcomed their new neighbours to Haliburton. Mary said "thank you, thank you so much." "Please come in". Mrs. Banks then introduced her family. "This is my husband Harry and this is my eldest child Preston and my youngest son Drew." Elizabeth introduced her family. "This is my husband Chris Henderson and our beautiful daughter Annabelle."

At that moment Preston spotted Annabelle and he felt his pulse quicken and his face heating up. Drew had spotted his brothers reaction and could not contain his comment. He looked at his mother and said "mom, look at Preston. He's in love." Preston proceeded to punch his little brother in the arm and Annabelle giggled to herself. She had remembered the boy sitting at the babbling brook and sure enough It was the shy boy standing in front of her now. She had thought he was cute but now she noticed that he was cuter than she had previously believed. He was looking at her and she could see that he thought that this young girl in front of him was adorable. Mrs. Henderson invited the Banks to come in and sit at the table. She offered to make tea or coffee, whichever they preferred, and they could share this gesture of friendship. They engaged in a wonderful conversation getting to know each other as the children played, and you could see Mr. Banks and Mr. Henderson, although from different paths, had both risen in their career with hard work and determination to give their families a better life. Mrs. Banks and Mrs. Henderson hit it off immediately. You could just feel that this would be something special.

Sometimes in life you meet someone or, in this case, two families, that begins a wonderful, friendship. You know that if you can come by it, you should be so lucky. This was one of those times. At the end of the night, the children had had so much fun, were exhausted and ready to go home. Although normally reserved, Preston had been smiling ear to ear and it was at this point you could already see he had found the girl that could possibly bring him out of his shell. As they were leaving, Mr. Banks reminded Mr. Henderson to be up and ready by 3:30 so they could go fishing and they both agreed that they would try out Mr. Henderson's new boat. When you think of how most friendships are started this wasn't so different than most. Very few friendships stand the test of time but when you have, as these two families, a bond that their children are soon to build and the adults as well, it is to wonderful to believe. That night Preston fell asleep with the thought of the new girl Annabelle and Drew had fallen asleep with the ridicule of his brother.

CHAPTER 6

WHILE HARRY AND CHRIS WERE fishing on Little Hawk Lake, their families were quietly sleeping. The men were enjoying each other's company and their love of fishing and at this point, you knew their bond would be strong. As the children woke in the morning, the two men were already enjoying the breakfast that Mrs. Henderson had made and when it comes to food that is already made, Mr. banks love of the Henderson's seemed that much greater. They were like two friends that had been fishing together for years.

The children rushed down to have their breakfast because they were ready to play with their new friend. The children were thinking of all the fun and of the many days of new adventures waiting ahead. They were ready to show the new friend they had made and even though Preston was a reserved young boy, he was also excited to show the adventures they could have in Haliburton. Zip lining, swimming, their treehouse and simply enjoying each other's friendship.

Later that morning, the ladies agreed to share their stories and tea. Mrs. Banks was describing her life before with Harry and the children. She told her Harry was a hardworking, great, supporting husband and father. She spoke about her children. Preston being the very reserved young man, but also a star soccer player in his little league and although he was much different then most boys his age, he was very deep for a child, best explaining him as smart with a quiet confidence. Drew however, was a fire cracker, searching out the next adventure and living every minute of his life with a smile. Drew had dark auburn hair where Preston was blond. Preston's idea of a fun time was reading a book whereas Drew was down for anything, dangerous or mischievous. Mrs. Henderson explained that Mr. Henderson was in many ways like Mr. Banks and to best describe her daughter she would say Annabelle was a little bit of both Preston and Drew. Mischievous, adventurous and reserved.

While the children were playing "hide and seek" they had all spotted their fathers coming back from their days fishing trip. Drew and Annabelle scampered to see their catch, while Preston simply took his time because his interest was not in fishing. Drew was happy, occasionally, to spend the day on the water with his father. He didn't mind getting worms out of the pail but Preston wasn't about putting any slimy thing on a hook and so he almost never joined his father on the boat. Although some dads would not be happy that his boy wasn't into what he liked, Mr. Banks loved that his oldest son was true to himself. He was proud that his boy was smart and he encouraged him to do what made him happy.

When they got there, to their amazement, the boat was full of fish and the men could not be prouder of themselves. The men said to their children, tonight, we are going to have a fish fry. Drew loved fish and Annabelle had never had fresh fish, but Preston loved to eat fish and was excited with the thought of a fish fry that night. The children had spent all day playing and were filthy, but Preston was at best slightly soiled because of course he would not engage in all the activities they did all day. At this point they had had a great day and although Preston wasn't as daring as his brother or Annabel, he joined in more than he would have if it was only himself and Drew. He wasn't about to sit back and let Drew be the whole life of the day though by this point Mrs. Henderson had called Annabelle.

Mrs. Banks called out to her boys and said go and get cleaned up as we are about to have our fish fry. Mr. Banks and Mr. Henderson were busy outdoors setting up their pots containing hot oil over an open fire. They couldn't be more excited to show what a good old fashioned fish fry looked like. They had engaged in a wonderful evening topped off by roasting marshmallows and making S'mores. When it came to roasting a marshmallow, no one made a more perfect roasted marshmallow than Preston as he had the most patience. Drew lost more in the fire pit then made it to the graham cracker, so they had let Preston be the pit-master. When he had been asked to make some for everyone, you could see the peacock strut and when it came to Annabelle he made certain that hers was perfect. The parents had noticed that their children, even at that age, had a special friendship, although they had just smiled and not made their children uncomfortable. The night was perfect and they stayed out until the next morning. They needed to get some sleep so they could do it all over in a few hours, and the children had fallen asleep in their parents' arms. The Banks and Hendersons thanked each other for making this a great night knowing this would be only one night of many in the days they would spend together.

The next two months of the summer were spent in joyful, rejoicing, fun filled days. That summer couldn't have been more blessed, with the first summer for the Henderson's at their new summer home enhanced by feeling like they had made friends with such wonderful neighbors like the Banks. They knew that their daughter had what must have been the best two months of her life and although Annabelle was a happy child she had been even more alive. They knew that coming here was not just great for them but they felt they had made the summer even more special for the Banks. It was the end of the summer and Drew was teasing his brother. "Hey Preston, are you not going to give your girlfriend a kiss before we leave?" Preston had wanted to punch his brother once again, however his father told him otherwise. So, Preston doing what he normally did when he was not comfortable, went to the spot where everything was peaceful and made his life easier to deal with.

Preston was indeed a loving complex young man who was different, unique. When he needed relaxation or thoughtful reflection, he had found a spot by the babbling brook that could be his special spot. There was a big old rock near the banks of the brook and he would often go there to find his thoughts and reflect because, in his mind, it was the most peaceful place on Earth. He would sit there sometimes reading a book and other times just reflecting. He loved the sound of the babbling brook and would wait for the winds to blow ever so softly and listen to the birds above singing such a lovely song.

That morning Annabelle had gone looking for Preston, to let him know it was the best summer of her life. He was the main reason for that. She looked everywhere: the treehouse, the swimming areas of the babbling brook and then she recalled the first day she had spotted him in the woods and of course that was where Preston was. She had wondered what he was doing there, he wasn't reading, just staring into the abyss and she wondered if she should disturb him at all because, even though she was a young girl, she was very thoughtful. But then her curiosity got the best of her. She had thought about turning around but she wanted to ask her new friend Preston what he was doing at the foot of the babbling brook. She proceeded to walk towards him and at that point Preston turned around and saw Annabelle coming toward him. Annabelle asked him if he was okay, and Preston simply said "yes of course, I am okay." I just come here, when I am sad or need time to myself." He went on to explain that when things feel too much for me, I sit here and listen to the babbling brook and feel its freshness. I wait for the winds to blow and the birds to sing. It is where I find my true happiness and as Annabelle looked at this boy she knew he was not like anyone she had ever meet before. She was lost in his eyes and just found herself listening and although Annabelle didn't understand she thought it was so sweet that a boy his age could be so deep.

At this point they could hear their parents yelling it was time to go, so they scampered back to where their parents were waiting at their vans. The Banks and Hendersons said "we will meet here again next year" and Mrs. Banks told Mrs. Henderson if they were not doing anything for the holidays maybe they could get together. Mary had a big smile on her face and said that would be wonderful. The next few days Annabelle talked to her mother and shared that she was fond of the Banks' boys. She liked Preston although she thought he was a little strange for a young boy, but she told her mother he was special in a good way. When Annabelle left, Mrs. Henderson sat at the table and called Mrs. Banks and told her what her daughter had shared. They both thought that it was precious and she knew that her son felt the same way and it was nice.

That year the Henderson's and the Banks had become closer and closer friends. They shared Thanksgiving and Christmas together and visited as much as they could. It was the start of a long-lasting relationship.

CHAPTER 7

THE NEXT SIX YEARS WERE FILLED with many happy summers, special occasions and holidays. The Banks and Hendersons and it became easier for the families to get along as Mr. Banks had also started to buy all his business vehicles from Mr. Henderson.

The children were always happy to share their lives together. They spent Halloween going out trick or treating together and you could see the young love between Preston and Annabelle blossoming. At this point, Annabelle and Preston had grown very fond of each other. They spent many nights talking and emailing each other about the events and days of their lives. Annabelle had matured into a young beautiful teenager, and Preston had grown up to be young and handsome. Make no mistake about it, their love was maturing right before their families lives. Although Preston rarely spoke of his feelings to his family, Drew made sure that everyone knew.

Drew loved to put his older brother on the spot, but in the last seven years he had also grown fond of Annabelle because she was more fun than his brother Preston. He knew that Annabelle looked at him like a kid brother and he was happy that Preston and Annabelle were fond of each other as well.

As the summer grew closer, Annabelle and Preston were so excited that once again they would spend the summer together but before they could start their summer, both Preston and Annabelle had grade school proms. Preston, being a very reserved child, was intimidated to ask Annabelle to be his date. Annabelle being the outgoing personality she was, had no problem asking Preston if he would accompany her to her grade school prom. At that point, Preston drew the courage to ask Annabelle if she would be his date and both couldn't have been any happier to do this for each other. Annabelle had her prom first. She told all her friends that her special friend, Preston, would be her date. Over the past few years, she had told them how wonderful Preston was and that he was not like most boys his age. He was kind and gentle. They had shared so much fun in their youth and her friends were enthralled and excited to finally meet Preston. Preston was excited at the prospect of attending each other's prom over the next two weeks, but he had not made much fuss over it. Drew, being Drew, would always tease him but Mrs. Bank and Mrs. Henderson could not have been more excited for their children. They had made so much fuss and were both more excited than their children.

The next two weekends were filled with young unadulterated love for Preston and Annabelle. They knew that soon they would spend their summer together once again. This summer changed because now Preston and Annabelle were about to take their relationship one step further and over the next few weeks a new chapter in their love began for Preston and Annabelle. Drew continued to make Preston uncomfortable in his own shoes. Mr. Banks enjoyed the ridicule of Preston by his younger brother. He would always tell Drew to be on his best behaviour and leave his old brother alone.

Now finally both the Banks and Hendersons were where they loved to be, in their cabins, in the woods of Haliburton. As usual, Mr. Banks and Mr. Henderson enjoyed the summer fishing and drinking together. Their friendship continued to flourish, building an even stronger bond. Mrs. Banks and Mrs. Henderson had also built a sisterhood. They loved to walk, garden and have morning and afternoon teas together. The evenings were spent together, both families enjoying cocktails, elaborate meals and conversations about everything, but at the heart of this unity was laughter and enjoyment. Drew had made some friends in the area and enjoyed his reckless youth through adventure and plain old fun.

Annabelle and Preston nurtured their ever-growing affection for each other and spent many days by the brook. Preston had often written and read poetry about Annabelle and their time together. It was young love, at its best. I call it innocent love, because there are very few distractions. Innocence is not spoiled when you are young. But as the summer ended, Preston, Annabelle and all the rest, got back to their regular routine. Preston and Annabelle knew they would see and talk to each other as frequently as they could. They knew deep down inside it was always better when they were at the cabins in Haliburton.

This year was going to be a new chapter in Preston and Annabelle young lives, as they would soon be spending more of their time studying. This would be the year they would enter high school, Preston at St Michael College for boys and Annabelle at St. Theresa's school for girls. The adventures they would have and their growth at the high school level would be fun, but they wouldn't be together. Drew, his father and Mr. Henderson himself would always tease Annabelle and Preston. They would say "look, two young love-struck lovers." Mr. Henderson would say, "when Preston is around Annabelle, he was a shy timid boy, even though he has been with her half of his life" and the ladies would simply say "leave them alone, because every woman would love to have a boy like Preston." The ladies often talked about how nice it would be if their children married one day. The men ignored the women's thoughts and had many nights and days of laughter and ridicule of their young children.

One night the fathers, under the influence of a few beers, had talked about how one day their children would get married. It would be two great families joining together and although the friendship they have built didn't depend on their children get married, it would make things even more perfect. They had finished off their last beers, walked each other to their cabins, knowing that they would see each other many times during the year. It was not the same here. It felt like he was here with a brother. Their relationship was special and they knew it was only a short year during which they would spend all the time with their families and each other. Maybe one day there would be grand kids and they both laughed and went in. Today was their last day and night before they would return to start new adventures.

As usual, Preston and Annabelle would walk hand and hand. Preston and Annabelle's favourite spot to do this was at the rock by the babbling brook. At this point, although they had been so mutually fond of each other, they had not yet ever shared their first kiss or truly ever expressed their feelings in words. Preston would never push himself in any way to disrespect Annabelle or her feelings. Preston, mumbling, brought out his courage. At this point his face was beat red and he grabbed Annabelle's hand and professed that he loved her. He had loved her from the first moment he saw her beautiful, kind, warm face. His heart was pounding and his hands were sweating, as Annabel professed her love and joy that he was in her life and that she will always love him, and hoped he would feel the same. When she was done, Preston hadn't said a word and Annabelle felt like she was going to die right there, if after all these years he hadn't felt the same way. It was at that moment Preston grabbed Annabelle with a loving grasp and pressed his lips on hers. Annabelle, felt she had wanted this moment for so long and wondered if Preston had felt the same but now that she knew the feeling was mutual it felt like their first kiss was heaven. It lasted so long they didn't hear Drew approach. Drew was standing behind them in pure amazement and shock, having been asked by his parents to retrieve them as it was time to go.

Preston knew that Drew would soon tell what he saw but, before Preston had a chance to stop him, Drew was scampering away to tell what he saw. Preston chased after his brother as fast as he could even though Drew had quite the head start and he was running hard and laughing even harder. Preston made one last attempt and dove at his brother's feet, but Drew was too quick. By the time he reached his parents and the Hendersons, he was out of breath. Gasping, Drew said to the Hendersons and the Banks, "I saw Preston and Annabelle kissing and it was a long kiss." The mothers let out a sigh and smiles that were brighter than any sun. Of course, the fathers chuckled to themselves and Drew joined in and as Preston and Annabelle came closer they saw and knew, that Drew had told them. Annabelle was not ashamed. It had been, in her young life, the most beautiful event with the boy she loved. It was simply worth remembering it and sharing it with her mother. Preston was not ashamed either as it felt so right, but if he could he would have kicked Drew's ass.

Both their parents simply smiled and Preston had felt relief, although he looked at Drew and told him

"I will get you back brother." When Annabelle made it back she had an angelic look and her father winked at Mr. Banks. Then he looked at Preston and asked him, as if he wasn't pleased, "well young man, what are your plans with my daughter?" Drew felt like he had gotten his brother in hot water. He wanted to step in and then Mr. Banks stopped Drew and let Mr. Henderson drill his son. He wanted to hear how his son would handle himself. He motioned to the women to stay out of it as well. Preston took a deep breath before he spoke, "Well sir, one day, when I am done my schooling, I will work at my father's company. I will work very hard and I will want a family. I would then like to ask for your beautiful daughter's hand in marriage and give her a happy life, like my father and you," Mr. Henderson. "That is my plan." Let's say the mothers were beside themselves, listening to this response. Annabelle and Drew had hugged him and the men just smiled. Mr. Henderson looked at his daughter and softly said "this is the only boy you can bring home." She looked at her father and smiled, bringing an end to another amazing summer.

CHAPTER 8

THE NEXT FEW YEARS WERE SPENT THE
same way, summering together in Haliburton with
holidays and free time was spent with the Banks and
Hendersons. The children had grown. Drew was in
his last year of grade school and Preston was in his
junior year in high school. Drew could hardly wait
to join his brother in high school so they could play
soccer once again on the same team. Preston was
excelling academically and on the soccer pitch, his
mind and heart were always on Annabelle.

Annabelle was also excelling at St. Theresa's, but
many days were spent reflecting on thoughts of the

boy that made everything better for her. She could not wait until the next time they would see each other. Although emailing and talking on the phone each night was great, it did not take the place of being together. It just wasn't the same.

Drew was also a great soccer player in school and would always say he couldn't wait to get to St. Michael's College to play with his big brother. He would say in his own words "reuniting the Banks boys and take on the world," followed with laughter.

Although Preston's heart was always with Annabelle, he had become very popular amongst his peers. He was an exemplary student and his teachers found Preston to be a pure joy and the years that he and Drew both attended St. Michael's College, they had won the soccer championship both years that he and Drew played together on the team. Preston was being recruited for scholarships across the nation, but Preston would not go anywhere unless Annabelle was to join him at the school. He probably could have been a significant asset to many pro teams, but he knew it would be hard on their relationship. Preston would not be able to live aboard without Annabelle so, when it came time for Preston and Annabelle to choose their preferred university, Preston made sure that he and Annabelle would be in the same school.

His brother and parents and the Hendersons had all told Preston, in no uncertain terms, that he should not turn down the opportunity to become a pro athlete but Preston was content with his future aspirations. He would be happy sharing his life with Annabelle, and with the prospect of taking over Banks' Pools and Hot Tubs. Although, they didn't understand Preston's choice, they would support it, because they understood Annabelle had become more than just a girlfriend.

He could not see himself in another country or school so far away. He knew inside that not being close enough to enjoy Annabelle everyday was not worth any scholarship or sport endeavour. But this summer, after their graduation, Annabelle and Preston planned to take a trip to Europe, back-packing. They still had not told their parents. Annabelle and Preston would let their parents know about their plans, before graduation, to explore Europe together before starting the arduous task of university.

Preston was going to study economics and finance. Annabel was going to study arts, because she had loved painting and her dream was to work one day in an art gallery or historical museum. They decided to gather together their families at Mr. Banks favourite Italian rest Mario's. They went to the restaurant that night and before going in, Mr. Banks had asked Preston, "what is the big celebration we are having tonight? So, glad you are paying." Preston smiled and told his dad," I'm using your credit card and Drew bust out laughing and so did Mr. and Mrs. Banks. They were so proud of their son's academic and athletic abilities, that they didn't mind footing the bill. When they were seated at the table, to their amazement, the Hendersons were there. Drew looked at his father and said "the bill just got bigger pops." During the meal, Preston was so anxious and nervous about telling his parents and Henderson's, that he and Annabelle wanted to spend the next two months travelling in Europe rather than going to the cottage in Haliburton. Annabelle, sensing that Preston was uncomfortable broaching the subject, went on to explain to their parents that she and Preston were going to take a trip to Europe before starting classes at the University of Springwater.

She went on to tell the families about their plans for the next two months and when she was done explaining the trip, the mothers were so supportive and figured it would be a wonderful time in their life. Mr. Banks didn't have much of an opinion, but Mr. Henderson kindly reminded Preston, "I'm not ready to be a grandfather so make sure, that I am not." Mr. Banks seconded that motion. Drew could only find humor in the thoughts of the adults and as usual, he ridiculed and found humour in the fact that his big brother and his "adopted" sister Annabelle were going to take a trip that he wished he could be very much a part of. The parents had shown contentment and wonderment that their children would experience this wonderful European trip together. They probably wished that they had done this in their youth and gave their children their blessings.

The next two weeks of their lives passed extremely fast. It was the eve of their European tour and Annabel and Preston had spent the whole evening talking about how they would go about experiencing every bit of their trip together including their journeys, sightseeing, savouring of many the many different foods and rejoicing in their love and appreciation for other cultures and of course each other. When the next morning came, Preston had his bags ready and of course the Banks would drive their son to the airport, and they planned to meet up at the Hendersons. Annabelle and Preston said goodbye to their families. Drew reminded him to bring some souvenirs. Their mothers, with tears streaming down their faces, watched them leave.

They boarded the plane for their Europe trip and when they settled in their seats he reached in and gave Annabelle a kiss. Annabelle looked at him and felt like there wasn't any other man in the world that could make her smile and excited just by his touch. She had the feeling that this trip was going to be the next step in their life and love together.

CHAPTER 9

IN THE NEXT FEW DAYS, THE BANKS and the Henderson's made their way up to their respective Haliburton cabins. They had initially felt somewhat depressed that Annabelle and Preston were not there with them, but they would soon move on and enjoy that summer as if the children were there. They often read emails from their children and felt as if they were a part of their journey.

Drew truly felt the loneliness without Annabelle and Preston, but he was looking forward to the next two months in the cabin at the lake. He was also looking forward to being the captain of the soccer team because his brother had moved on, and it was up to him to continue to make the Banks' name known as true stars on the soccer team.

Annabelle and Preston had started their European trip in England and had taken in all the sites that tourist normally do. They also visited some shady pubs. They found that the people were so different but they knew that they lived in small towns. They jumped from place to place, living their lives and doing it together. It was just the start but, thanks to their parents, they had a chance to do this now and having a good laugh or two they enjoyed their time in England. They took in all the famous sites and now they where ready for the next place.

They travelled to Portugal where they enjoyed both the food and the culture. One day they had been invited to a beach party that the locals were throwing for a guest that stayed in the same hotel where they were staying. They had seen that the customs of these people, who in Preston's mind had so much less then he had, showed the true sense of happiness. It is not about how much money you have or the clothes that you wear. It was about just being with friends, having one big party, sharing food, drink, music and conversation. He noticed that Annabelle too was enjoying herself. She felt like one of them. She danced and drank and engaged in many celebrations with both locals and tourists alike. They travelled to many islands with Annabelle embracing all she had seen and just watching her having fun had made Preston enjoy this trip more than he even thought possible. He noticed how beautiful she looked in the sunset the last night in Portugal. It was the closest they had come to taking the next step in their lives. The mood was right and the moon was bright but he wasn't sure, so he waited. Annabelle was ready but she was going to wait until he made the first move. For now, she was happy to sleep in bed with the man she loved.

The next day, when they got to France, they were overwhelmed with all the wonderful smells that lurked around every corner. They had travelled to the Eiffel tower, kissed in the moonlight and enjoyed their walks through the Riviera. They enjoyed the many nights of their tour of France, sampling sweets and indulging in lovely coffee, with spirts. They rented a cottage on the Amalfi coastline as their destination, overlooking the beautiful turquoise waters. It proved to be the most wonderful experience of the trip. They spent the next two weeks there and dove deep into the culture of the Italians as they travelled the coastline. They said to each other that one day when they get married they should come back here. Annabelle looked at him and asked "you thinking of getting married to me?" and Preston looked at her and replied "you are the only one that I ever think about since the first day I saw you. I have never thought about spending my life with anyone else "and before he had a chance to say another word, she kissed him. They enjoyed every minute of the trip and as Annabelle and Preston would say in their own words the food was simply divine and they wished they had two stomachs each. They thought to themselves that this was the most beautiful place on Earth and could not help being caught up in the romance. The actuality was, Preston could not fight the feelings he had inside. They had been together for many years, only sharing kisses and now Preston was in denial. It was time to experiment and experience each other in all the love they shared. He had always kept those thoughts in the back of his mind. He was a gentleman and he recalled the statement that

Mr. Henderson had left him with, "In no uncertain terms am I ready to be a grandfather," and with that Preston chuckled. Anabelle herself wondered when would be the time, that she would feel Preston's love. They were both inexperienced but had often thought they could not bear to spend their life without each other.

They spent their last night in Italy dining at Alfredo's Seafood House. Preston ordered oysters having heard that they were an aphrodisiac. Annabelle had an mischievous smile on her face, as if she knew why Preston had ordered the oysters. If he would have only made the first move, the oysters would not have been necessary as the atmosphere and wine would have been enough. She would ultimately be with the man, she would undoubtedly spend rest of her life with. Annabelle looked at Preston and hoped that tonight he would make the first move. She knew deep down inside he was a gentleman but she hoped wholeheartedly that he would not be tonight. She could not control the feelings inside her as well. She was lusting for him. She wanted to feel him deep inside her, to feel their bodies as one. They got back to their room and they went outside with a bottle of Brig, and he poured her a glass. He was a true gentleman. He gave her the first taste and then he proceeded to put the bottle down and went over and played a song. Ti'Amo.

In Annabelle's mind, she was not aware that it was at this point that Preston threw his inhibitions to the wind. He walked around the table and reached for her hand and asked her if she would dance with him. He started kissing the nape of her neck and she was in heaven. Enthralled, she could feel the moisture within her. Her body aching to be devoured and before she knew it Preston had picked her up off her feet. Ever so gently he walked to the bed and started taking off her clothes one button at a time. He caressed her, at first her breasts, ever so gently because he wanted to be a gentleman. Annabelle wanted him to be an animal, to take her in his arms and ravish her repeatedly until she squealed in the night. They made love it was the greatest night of their young love. Preston had been gentle but firm and showed her love like she always thought it would be. They continued to make love all night long ending with both climaxing together like they did everything else. They had made love for the first time and in both their minds it could not have been any more special. It was unbridled love and so true to the core of its existence it could only have come from their lives.

They had finally taken their love to the next level. They laid in each other's arms feeling they had given each other something truly special. Unlike most first time experiences in the world of young love, it wasn't rushed nor would they relate their story as a conquest. No, this was true love. Not only had they shared each other's virginity, but it was special. The action of love not sex.

CHAPTER 10

ANNABEL AND PRESTON HAD SHARED an amazing night and it would not be their last, but now they had to get back to reality, to Midhurst and to Springwater University. The Banks and the Hendersons were not excited either as they knew summer was coming to an end. They knew that there would be many more summers in their future but it wasn't the same as the other years, because their son and daughter where not at the cottage this time. Even though Drew and some of his friends had come to stay, it wasn't the same.

It was now time to pick up the children from the airport. Drew was excited to see Preston and Annabelle. He had always given his brother a tough time that was just who Drew was. He had also known he loved his brother and he couldn't be happier with the blossoming relationship between Annabelle and Preston. Drew wondered if his brother and Annabelle had had a great time in Europe and even if they had more than a very good time. He laughed so hard that he had made himself cry. Mr. Banks looked back at his son in the rear-view mirror and asked "why are you crying?" Drew wasn't going to let him know what the real reason was, so he told his dad he was looking forward to seeing his brother and Annabella. Mr. Banks knew he was lying and told him to stop it. He did stop because, to be honest, he had missed his brother and Annabelle. He felt it was good that his brother had laid the ground work in both school and sport for him so, as he got older, he could go away. He was looking forward to that day but for now, seeing them again would be just enough.

When they arrived at the airport, Preston and Annabelle were waiting to see their families and as soon as they went through customs, there they were.

The Banks, the Henderson's and his pain in the ass brother Drew. On the ride, back from the airport, Annabelle and Preston told them what a wonderful experience travelling across Europe had been. They couldn't believe how beautiful Italy was. Annabelle's mother had asked "is it true that there is romance in the air in the Amalfi coastline?" Drew looked at his brother and saw Preston keep his head down. Drew knew they had shared intimacy, but Preston would never speak of it. They spent that night together, two families together as one. They had a great time sharing all the events that had happened at their cabin and on the European trip.

The next morning the Henderson and the Bank's households were in complete chaos because it would be the first day for both Annabelle and Preston at Springwater University. They both would live in residence on campus. Annabelle's father, Chris, had reminded them that they would live in separate residences and not together. Mr. Henderson could only imagine to himself that his young daughter was not so pure anymore but as a father, it was not a thought he should focus on. The Banks and the Hendersons made their way to Springwater

University and got their kids set up in their own dorm rooms.

The lives of the Hendersons and the Banks would be different once again as their children were growing up and attending university. They would only be home for the holidays or when the parents made surprise visits to the university. Mrs. Banks cried as she left her son. As a mother, it was hard to let go. He would not need her as much anymore. She was glad that Drew still needed her because life with Drew would never be boring and that was a comfort to her. Mr. Banks reminded his son that this was the proudest moment of his life. His son was in university, something he himself wasn't given the opportunity to do. Mrs. Henderson was nervous. She knew it was something that Annabelle had to do. She was proud that Annabella would make something of her life by attending university but she would always remain her little girl.

Over the next few weeks and months, Annabelle and Preston got accustomed to their new surroundings. They enjoyed the thought of being together and studying. Promiscuous actions were enjoyed almost as if they were already married.

They had made many friends in a short time at the university. The transition was much easier than they had ever thought. Springwater had made it to the soccer semi-finals for the first time in the fifty-year history of the school. Preston was enjoying all that the university had to offer, but most of all that his sweetheart Annabelle was always close. Annabelle could not have been any more pleased with her courses. Her teachers said she had a real talent for art. She enjoyed all the knowledge she gained through the life experiences of being for most part on her own, yet having the comfort of having the man she loved always close by her side.

Over the next two years they had many successes academically, athletically and socially at university. Drew himself had led St. Michael College to two more championships. He was the most popular kid around. He had all his brother's physical attributes but, unlike Preston, he enjoyed and embraced the life of not only being a great soccer player but also the class clown and a true partier as his friends called him. The Banks and Hendersons had spent a great deal of time together over last two years, but the families enjoyed Haliburton the best, as this was the time the families could be together.

They had built a wonderful, fourteen-year friendship that felt like they had been friends, like their children, since a very young age. The prospect that their children, Preston and Annabelle, would one day unite and make a family was in the Banks and Henderson women's thoughts but was rarely in the those of the men. It was unbelievable that two years had flown by so rapidly. Could life be anymore, perfect?

This year at the cabin in Haliburton was very special for Drew because, he too, was going to join the ranks with his brother and Annabelle at Springwater University. He had many scholarship offers abroad but, like his brother, he made a choice to stay close to his brother and potential sister-in-law. He told his parents and anyone who would listen, that he could not wait to reunite the dual soccer team of the Bank's brothers. Together, Preston and Drew would rule the soccer world. His parents could not have been happier. The next week would be Drews' graduation prom and he was going with the hottest girl in school. In his words, "why not? She gets to go with me, Drew Banks."

The day after Drew's graduation would be the start of the summer holidays. They went to Springwater to pick up Preston and Annabelle for the summer extravaganza in Haliburton. Mr. Banks was sitting at the dinner table. He looked at his wife and let her know that he was the luckiest man in the world, even thou his father-in-law still wasn't his biggest fan. He thanked her for marrying him and for raising two boys that had made a life filled with the most wonderful memories. Drew walked in at that moment and Mr. Banks stood up to embrace his son. Drew answered "dad, I love you too "and that had touched Mrs. Banks. She told Mr. Banks that she was the lucky one and that's when they gave each other a loving kiss. Drew looked and said "I can't take this. I'm out of here."

CHAPTER 11 DREW'S DAY

MR. AND MRS. BANKS WERE SITTING around the breakfast table. They could not believe where the time had gone. Preston was in his second year at university and Drew was graduating high school. They couldn't have been more proud of their boys. They felt on top of the world. Mr. Banks simply said to Mrs. Banks "you have been a wonderful wife and mother. You should be very proud of yourself that our boys have grown up to be respectful and good boys well most of the time for Drew anyways." Today was Drew's graduation. Drew came back down and asked if the gross stuff between his parents was over.

He, himself had come downstairs to kiss his mother on the cheek. He slapped his dad on the back and told his parents "I'm graduating and I'm going to join Preston at Springwater University. I can't be any happier that I am going to the prom tonight with the hottest chick in school." Mrs. Banks simply shook her head, and Mr. Banks smiled. Later that day Preston and Annabelle were making their way to St Michael to be part of Drew's graduation festivities. The Hendersons also made sure they would be there to celebrate Drew's graduation festivities with the Banks. Drew had no idea his brother or Annabelle were going to be there. He only knew his brother and Annabelle were going to be picked up and head off to the cabin in Haliburton the next day.

As the festivities went on with the graduation, it was time for Drew to receive his diploma. He noticed his parents, the Hendersons and to the right of father his brother were Preston and Annabelle, all of whom could not be more proud. At the end of the graduation ceremony Drew made a b-line for his brother first and gave him a big hug. He shared his excitement about the upcoming summer and the prospect of their reunion, of their soccer supremacy together at the University of Springwater next fall. He also mentioned to his brother and family that he was looking forward to the best part anyone is ever going to have, a graduation prom night. He said goodbye to everybody and thanked the Hendersons for coming to see him graduate. He told his brother once again how much he looked forward to being with he and Annabelle this summer and at school for the next few years. Preston reminded his brother to give them hell and have a great time. Drew looked back at his brother, a brother he loved and respected.

That night Drew had taken his date, his high school sweetheart Ashley Summers, to the prom. They danced all night, partied with their friends and laughed about all their high school memories. This was the greatest party they had been to up to this point. Unknown to his friends or to Ashley, no one had noticed how much alcohol and weed Drew had consumed by the end of the night and Drew wasn't done partying yet. He asked all his closest friends, their dates and Ashley, when they had gathered outside around their cars, if they wanted another drink. They sat around and saw Drew get into his car and take out a cooler. While he passed around more beers his friends were telling Drew to slow down. They were, at this point, all ready to go home. Drew was talking and joking. He was being the guy they all knew. He was happy and wasn't ready to call it a night. When they had consumed all the beer, Drew wanted this one night to always be remembered, so he begged his friends to take the party to the bluffs just outside of town. Drew and Preston had spent most of their childhood playing and diving off the cliffs and It was one of his favourite places to go. Drew and Preston had, had fun jumping from the highest parts of the cliffs, especially on hot summer days. Although his friends were against going to the bluffs and continuing to party, Drew was very persuasive. After all, they all wanted to be a part of the last party of high school. They knew if they didn't go, Drew would be pissed at them and if it was their idea, Drew wouldn't think twice about doing what they wanted, so they made their way up to the bluffs. They made a fire and Tommy, Drew's closest friend, had brought a few bottles of alcohol and an ounce of cannabis. Through the wee hours of the night they continued drinking, smoking and having a great time.

It was at this point that many if his friends were ready to go home, including Tommy. Drew, being Drew, persuaded them to wait because he had to make one more jump before they all went home. Drew did not realize the danger of making this jump in his befuddled state. Although Tommy was persistent in trying to stop Drew from jumping, in the end, he knew that Drew would make up his own mind and do whatever he wanted. Drew made his way to the highest point on the bluffs where he and Preston had made the jump many times before and despite the countless screams from Tommy and Ashley not to jump Drew just laughed and kidded with them. He had made this jump 1,000 times before with Preston. They yelled at him, "You are drunk and stoned. You cannot make this jump," and with once last breath Drew looked at his friends and said "you watch while a drunk, stoned man makes this jump you chicken shits." As Drew made the jump his friends couldn't believe that Drew had actually jumped. As Drew began to dive he yelled "this is amazing." To their surprise, when they ran to the cliff to see their friend, he had made the jump. Looking into the water they could not see Drew swimming about until Tommy spotted Drew's lifeless body on the jagged rocks below the cliffs. They ran down and when they got there they looked at Drew laying on the rocks. He wasn't moving and bent down to see if he was dead. They could not believe he was dead. They all broke down crying and Tommy yelled out for someone call 911. As they all wiped their tears, they came to the realization they had lost their friend and decided It would be left to Tommy to call Mr. Banks. A few minutes later, after placing the call Paramedics, Police and Firemen had all arrived as fast as they could. They examined the body and quickly came to the realization there was no chance to save this young boy's life. Police questioned all the children when they had settled them down, and the group of friends explained what had happened. It was an easy situation for the police to investigate. It was a bunch of friends parting after their graduation and one of the young men, showing off, lost his life. The worst part was going to be telling the parents. The police wondered and then asked one simple question. "Why didn't you try to stop him?" and Tommy said "when Drew makes up his mind, there is nothing anyone can do to change it."

Just then, accompanied by the Hendersons, the Banks arrived at the scene. Mr. Banks ran so fast that he fell and was helped to his feet by a police officer. The policeman asked who he was and he said "I'm the boy's father." The police simply looked at him and said "I'm sorry. I think it's better that you don't go down there." Mr. Banks said "I have to. I need to see him with my own eyes. He was just alive a few hours ago and now he is dead." After seeing his son's broken body, he went up to explain to his wife. She was motionless and fell to the ground. Mr. Henderson could only hold her. What do you say to a mother who has lost her child? Someone that she had cared for, nurtured and loved, only to have him taken away. Why? You believe you have raised them to use common sense yet still, for the thrill of life, they forget that they have someone who will suffer their death even longer than the life they have lived. Mrs. Banks brought herself back to the realization of what had happened. Mr. Banks was so angry and overwhelmed that he resisted the consoling from his friend, Mr. Henderson. When he saw the group of Drew's friends, he jumped right in front of them and asked "How did this happen? Why didn't you stop him? Why didn't you call me before he did it?" Although most of the children were still weeping and trying to come to grips with what happened, he grabbed Tommy because he knew he was Drew's best friend. He grabbed him in such a violent way it was a wonder how Tommy didn't get whiplash. Tommy started to weep again saying "I know it's not the same for a best friend to lose his friend as it is for a father to lose his son." It was at that point Mr. Banks understood that his son was gone. His pride and joy, his boy and life would never be the same. His heart hurt too much and he fell to his knees, with tears streaming down his eyes, and yelled "I wish I was a better father and stopped my son from being the free spirit that he was." He wanted to give his boy the life he wanted as a boy and once again cried out "My beautiful boy. Why God? Was he so bad? Was I so bad? Look at my wife. You have broken her heart." He went to his wife" Get up honey, it's time to go home. Our son is gone. No, our son is dead." As the Banks and Hendersons left for home there wasn't one dry eye. A tough nosed cop looked at one of the other cops and said "it was such a loss of a young man with big dreams and even an bigger heart." It's so hard to believe that a night of fun snuffed it all out, never to come home again." When they arrived home, they were so overwhelmed that they decided not to call Preston that night.

Mr. and Mrs. Banks, crawled into bed and cried the night away. They would have to deal with burying their youngest son. Buy a grave site, a casket and he would have to tell Preston in the morning that his younger brother, the one that had looked forward to reuniting the Banks boys at Springwater University, was simply gone. Mrs. Banks spent the rest of the night in and out of sleep. She would often go into Drews bedroom and lay on his bed. She would smell his pillows to bring her the memory of her boy. It was so hard for her to believe that her son was gone. It was hard for her to admit it was his time and it was not her fault he had jumped. Drew lived his life to the fullest everyday and that was what she was going to remember. Every time she had been down he had brought a smile to her face and with that she fallen asleep.

During her restless sleep, at some point during the night, she had a dream, that Drew had come to her with his smiling face. He had always done this before. He assured his mother that he was doing well and he was in a much better place. He would look forward to the day she would join him, but not too soon. Drew told his mother to be strong, not only for herself, but for dad and Preston because he was in a far better place, up in Heaven. The winds were blowing, the birds singing and the babbling brook was running. She should always remember that he was there right at his favorite place. This should keep you smiling when you stand there and think of me. Tell Preston that I'm sorry that I have let him down, but that he will always be in my memory. He could not have asked for a better brother and not to be worried about him. To remember that he lived his life with a smile and joy in his heart. Although he had done something stupid, he had lived his life in happiness. He will be watching Preston and although they are hurting now, remember that the love he had gotten from them all was enough for ten lifetimes. Mom, tell dad I love him and I heard what he had said to God and its not God's fault our yours. It was mine. I loved being your son. Mom I love you and one day we will stand side by side again. It is only good-bye for now.

CHAPTER 12

THE NEXT MORNING THE BANKS WERE sitting around the table. They knew they had to go to St. Jude's, the funeral home, but it was so hard for them to leave the table. Mom had made bacon and eggs, Drew's favourite. She even set his plate. Mr. Banks reminded her that he was not here anymore and almost simultaneously they broke down. They cried and they embraced. They knew that Drew would never be back. They thought of all the memories of their little boy, playing in the backyard, always so dangerously close to the edge of the pool. Mrs. Banks, at times, would chase him away with a broom. The memory of Drew at the cabin in Haliburton and how he would be filled with joy just to be there and play with his brother. They still couldn't believe that their little boy was gone. That instead of driving to the cabin in Haliburton, they had to plan their boy's funeral. It was all so hard to take but they knew it had to be done. They got cleaned up and drove to St. Jude's. They sat down with the mortician who was so kind. Knowing he had done this before, he asked the Banks how they would like the funeral done. Mr. and Mrs. Banks said "we want to give our son a great send off. "Mr. Oliver, the mortician, said he understood that it had been a very hard day and they appreciated his understanding. Mr. Oliver said "I have children of my own and although I do this for a living, to bury one of your own, I can't even imagine." Once all the documents and contracts were signed. Mr. and Mrs. Banks thanked Mr. Oliver. They knew now they must go and tell Preston the horrific news, so off they went to Springwater University. Mrs. Banks had asked the Hendersons to meet them at the school and not tell Annabelle before they had a chance to let Preston know about the passing of his brother. The Hendersons obliged. On the way to the school to tell Preston, they heard over the radio, the report on what had happened at the bluffs and the fact it was their son had died was overwhelming. They couldn't believe what tragedy had happened to their son Drew. Mr. Banks said "I have heard of so many people who have lost their children but to really know how it feels is to live in their shoes. You never think of your children dying before you. It has to be the worst thing a parent can go through."

Mr. Banks said to Mrs. Banks "I'm not sure how we are going to break the news to Preston." Drew was very strong, but Preston was more emotional. They remembered the time when Preston was a boy and his pet turtle had passed, he hadn't talked for three weeks. They wondered to themselves how they could we make it easier on Preston, because it is not a turtle, it's his kid brother. When they finally got to the university, the Hendersons were already waiting for them. Mrs. Henderson asked "what would you like us to do?" Mrs. Banks said to Mary, "you go and tell Annabelle and um, we will go see Preston." Although they had lost Drew, they couldn't imagine how it would go telling Preston.

When they finally reached the dorm room they knocked on his door. Preston was in the shower so Mike, his roommate and best friend, answered the door. "Mr. and Mrs. Banks, what are you doing here? We still have a week of school." They smiled and asked Mike where Preston was. Mike had noticed that something was different this time. Mr. Banks would generally break his balls, but today he stood in the doorway with a blank look on his face. He asked them to come in and offered them a water and left-over Mac and Cheese. They said "no thanks. Could you please call Preston?" Mike knocked on the bathroom door and said "your parents are here." Preston thought that was odd. They came to visit me earlier. He yelled at Mike "tell them I will be out in a minute." The Banks sat down on the bed, waiting for their son. Mike could see something was wrong. Preston came out, smiled at his parents and looked at Mike. Preston said "Mike, my parents love me so much they came to visit me, even though it's a week away from the end of the term." At this point, Preston hadn't noticed his parent's eyes were red and puffy, but Mike had noticed Mrs. Banks was not herself. She usually had a smile on her face and always brought enough baked goods for both boys to enjoy. Preston said to his mother and father, "it's nice to see you, but it's only a couple of days until summer. Have you missed me that much?" When Preston looked at his parents faces once more, he knew something was wrong and they had not just come for a visit. Mr. Banks looked at Preston and he could see the tears forming in his eyes. "Preston we have some terrible news." Preston asked "what is it Mom and Dad? Is something wrong with one of you guys? Is something wrong with Drew, dad?" Mr. Banks, tears streaming down his cheek, stood up and grabbed Preston's hand and said "son, your brother has passed away." Preston stood still, like he never heard a thing, then before he had a chance to react, the door flung open and Annabelle was hysterical. She said "Drew is dead!" All Preston said was "Oh My God, mom how? How did he die?" and at that time, the Henderson's entered the room. They sat by the Banks on the bed and watched Annabelle and Preston cry hysterically. Preston was hoping it was a dream, but he pinched himself and knew it wasn't.

When Preston and Annabelle composed themselves, the Banks could not speak, so Mr.

Henderson explained. Drew was partying all night with his friends, having a great old time, when Drew decided to go to the Bluffs. Later his friends had tried to persuade him to leave, but by that time Drew was too drunk and stoned. You know how your bother is when he makes up his mind to do something. He does whatever he wants. He had dared his friends to come to the top of the bluff, at the highest point, to jump with him. His girlfriend was crying telling him not to do it but Drew wasn't listening. He jumped. He landed on the rocks, his body nothing but a lifeless broken entity. When Mr. Henderson was finished telling Preston, he was in shock. He had lost his brother, his best friend. He remembered the last words he spoke with his brother, how it was Drew and Preston's dream to once again reunite the Banks brothers on the soccer pitch and now that was gone. Preston had broken down screaming at the top of his lungs, "why Drew, why Drew, why Drew?" It was so hard for the Banks, the Hendersons and Annabelle to see how broken and sad Preston was currently. Over the next hour Annabelle and Preston gathered their things, Preston still in shock. He gave his captains sleeve to Mike and told him" I'm not coming back." Mike wasn't going to say anything right now. He figured Preston was just upset and once he dealt with the loss of his brother he would be back. They got in their cars and headed for home. As they drove off, Preston's eyes still full of tears, he looked back at the university and he knew life, as he knew it, could not and would not be the same again. It had pained him to think that his brother Drew would never kick a soccer ball or they would never enjoy the cabin again.

Life without his brother would never be the same. Preston looked back at the University of Springwater and knew he would never be back. He could never see himself back at the school. He felt that he would look at the pitch and wonder why his brother wasn't there. When Drew died, Preston's passion for the game was no longer there anymore. He turned around and closed his eyes. He didn't want to see anything and at that point his head ached too much. Annabelle went to hold his hand and that was the first time he pulled his hand away. She thought that she should give him space and time to grieve.

CHAPTER 13

LATER THAT DAY THE BANKS ARRIVED home. They asked the Hendersons to join them as they didn't want to be alone. The Henderson's obliged, they were part of the family. When they got home, Mrs. Banks started cooking and Mrs. Henderson helped. Mr. Henderson and Mr. Banks sat in the garage and Mr. Banks brought out a bottle of bourbon. He felt the need to drink his sorrows away and Mr. Henderson obliged. Mr. Henderson comforted his dear friend. He was there to be a shoulder to cry on.

As the women were busy making the meal, Preston had gone to sit in Drew's room. He was looking at all the photos Drew had in his room. Preston had noticed that the pictures were of him and the notes his brother had written brought a smile to his face. He knew that his brother was a fan, but this was love. He hurt even more when Annabelle came through the door to join him. Preston looked over all his brother's belongings, bringing back many childhood memories. They loved to play Cowboys and Indians. Preston stared at all the board games they had played while growing up.

Looking at Annabelle, with his eyes full of tears, he told her that it was all his fault. She stated "what are you talking about?" He went on to say," I should have stayed and kept an eye on my brother because I knew he was going to party. We all knew how Drew was." She answered him as delicately as she could. "How could you have known that he would jump?" "I know my brother. He's a care free soul. He always wanted to be the life of the party and never had any boundaries. He would always act first and think later." Annabelle said, "you couldn't always be there to protect your brother." "You couldn't have known he would make the choice to jump." I know it is hard to see that, but Drew always looked for adventure and he was the only one could stop himself." Preston knew deep down inside what Annabelle was saying was all true he couldn't stop thinking if he had been there to chaperone his brother, all of this would not have happened. He couldn't stop himself from feeling guilty. It was so hard to say goodbye. He felt that they had so much life to live and he looked forward to his brother joining him at Springwater University. He could see in his mind, number eight and number twelve, soccer players, running rickshaw all over the country together. They would have hoisted the championship trophy. Together. He could see the smile on Drew's face. A lion on the field, the heart a true lover of all, a great friend to most and a kid brother to me. Annabelle started crying. She had never heard Preston talk with such emotion. She had known it was in him. Why did he wait, to express it? It had taken so many years to let everyone know how he truly feels. She thought to herself, it was funny how, in times like this, people had no trouble finding their true self. Preston just sat there looking through his brother's things. Annabelle herself, not having any siblings, had looked at Drew like a kid brother. She wished she would have had siblings, but she loved him like a brother.

She remembered, fondly, the times that the three of them would play in the treehouse for hours and hours, swimming in the brook, just the three of them, all summer long. Preston would always be the prudent one, wanting to go back, but he would always do what it took to keep his brother and Annabelle smiling. She had remembered when she was the prisoner in their game of Cowboys and Indians. Drew would take her as hostage, and Preston would always be her saviour. She had fond memories of sitting around the fire pit in the summers making S'mores and hot dogs. She remembered the time Drew had eaten ten hotdogs and then stuffed four S'mores in his mouth. Preston, like a mother, would warn him he would be sick, and sure enough Preston was right, and the three of them would all laugh. She loved just being part of their family. The Christmas's they spent together. Drew's excitement and joy, waking up early and calling everyone down to the tree. He would open every present with laughter and happiness. She suffered the realization that Drew would no longer be there anymore. When Preston sat back down on the bed, he looked at Annabelle and gave her a hug. He told her "I have been so self-absorbed in losing my brother, I haven't even stopped to think how it makes you feel. I know how you felt about Drew and I know he loved you too." I had often thought of taking vacations one day when Drew married and our children could play together. "How could Drew be so selfish?" he said to Annabelle. "He took his life and he also took that with him. I can't bear to think that my life must go on, and that my little brother will not be here to share any more adventures." They both started crying. Annabelle said "I know, but we must continue. Drew would want us to." They embraced and went downstairs to join their families for dinner. That night the Hendersons would stay to support the Banks in their time of need. It had been a long day for Preston and Annabelle and they curled up on the couch, watching television, and that's where they fell asleep. Mrs. Banks and Mrs. Henderson covered their kids with blankets and tucked them in.

As they went upstairs Mrs. Banks went into Drew's room again. She remembered how fondly she was of her baby, Drew. She recalled many bedtime stories. Up till today, Drew would always wait for his mother to tuck him in. Tonight, there would be no Drew, only a room and a house full of memories, a mother weeping with a broken heart, knowing her little boy would not come home again.

The next morning, they got themselves ready. It had been a tough evening for Preston and Annabelle and today would be the public viewing of Drew. It was very sombre in the home. You couldn't even hear a pin drop while they ate breakfast. Once they were done, they got ready. It was going to be a long day for the Banks and Hendersons at St. Jude's Funeral Home. As Mr. Oliver, had promised, the room was filled with flowers. There were many telegrams from distant friends and family members. They looked at all the flowers and pictures of a life that was lost so young. There were so many pictures of the family and there wasn't one that Drew hadn't had a smile or that he wasn't laughing. That was how they would remember him. They thought that he was already raising hell in heaven and even though it was heart breaking, they found humor in the fact that no matter where Drew went, he could bring happiness. They read all the telegrams and looked at the beautiful flowers that had been sent for their boy, but it hadn't made the day any easier to deal with. It was, however, a very nice gesture that the well-wishers sent.

It was not yet one p.m. and Mr. Oliver had asked if they were ready to receive the condolences and well wishes for Drew. The line stretched all the way outside and wrapped around the building including thousands of friends, school mates and family. The Banks were overwhelmed by all the support. Mrs. Banks said to Mr. Banks, "Drew was truly loved" although this didn't make them feel any better. Annabelle stood beside Preston as streams of people offered their condolences. Preston, with a blank expression on his face, tried his best to accept their well-meaning condolences. He thought to himself that, although this was nice, it would not bring my brother back. Annabelle held his hand through all of it. Preston knew that she had been suffering too, he couldn't imagine anyone more wonderful than her. Even though her unwavering support was truly appreciated, his heart was broken in two. He thought he should be strong for his mother and father, but deep down inside he was broken. He couldn't bear to think that soon his brother would be buried, how life would be without Drew. He hated himself. He hadn't done more to be by his brother's side. What was he supposed to do? Was he supposed to hang on his brother? Was he to stay by his brother's side, walk him across every road for the rest of his life? He felt that in some way, he should have talked more to his brother and told him that sometimes you need to sit back and think before you act. He also knew that Drew would do whatever he wanted. He remembered that family is the place where life begins and in death, as in life, love never ends.

He knew his brother's theory in life was live for today and make it so beautiful that every moment, of everything you do, is worth remembering. We are not here for a long time, Drew would say, but live every day like it is worth remembering and for a few minutes in the last couple days, Preston had a smile on his face. He felt as though he was floating on air, that it was not real, that Drew would pop out of the coffin and yell out it is time to party, Drew is here. Preston knew that was not the way it was going to be. It was nine p.m. in the evening when, finally, the last well-wishers had come and gone. Mr. Oliver entered the room and as delicately as he could, he asked the Banks and other family members, if they could pay their last respects. Tonight, was the night the coffin would be closed forever. All their family had gone through the parlor, the Hendersons next, as tears fell down Mary and Chris' face, they too had loved Drew. They remembered all the smiles that he had brought to their lives and couldn't imagine how the Banks truly felt. When they left, their eyes were full of tears. Next it was Preston and Annabelle. Preston's hands were shaking, he felt that anytime his legs would give out, but he knew he had Annabelle holding him tight. In his hand, he held a note. In the note, he had written, To my loving brother. I will always miss you. Home is where our story begins, and I will try to remember the message you always said. Live well, laugh often, love much. Brother, a part of my heart will be buried with you. It is hard today, to see the light, for you have cast a shadow of darkness. Although, I know you lived more in eighteen years than most people live in a hundred, this is not goodbye. I will see you another time. Your loving brother Preston. He could barely lift himself up from the stool in front of his brother's coffin, with Annabelle's help he walked out the door. He couldn't bring himself to look once more but Annabelle looked and blew Drew a kiss and said "I love you." When Mrs. And Mr. Banks approached the coffin of their son, they never imagined that they would bury one of their children before themselves. The thought of two parents looking upon their dead son and having to say goodbye was the worst nightmare of their lives.

Mr. Oliver extended a hand to the Banks and simply said "it was a tragic loss and I hope one day you will find peace." Mr. Oliver, with that said, closed the coffin. The next morning had finally come. The hole was dug, and Drew was laid where he would rest in peace. As Drew was lowered into his plot, tears streamed all around. There must have been two thousand people. There wasn't one dry eye in sight. Preston had stood far back. He didn't want to watch his brother being lowered. Annabel stood by his side, clutching his hand tightly, letting him know she was there. She could never take the place of his brother and would never do so. When the funeral was done and Drew laid to rest, Mr. Oliver had reminded all the guests, there was a buffet lunch with coffee and tea, for those who could attend. Although most people had left, the closest friends and family members were there to give their best and out of respect to the Banks. It had been a long day and the family couldn't wait for it to end. After they were done, they had driven home. All Preston and his parents could think of was Drew and the fact he would not be joining them. This was the saddest day of the Banks life.

CHAPTER 14

ONE WEEK LATER, THE BANKS AND Hendersons had gone up to their cabins in Haliburton. It was a new beginning, the saddest chapter in their lives. This was the first time the Banks had been there without Drew. Preston did not want to be there, but he obliged Annabelle and his parents. Mr. Henderson and Mr. Banks continued their love of fishing and companionship while Mary and Elizabeth did what they both loved, enjoying tea, gardening and the outdoors.

Preston had a much more difficult time. It was hard for Annabelle because she felt that Preston kept her at bay. He was not the loving and affectionate man she had grown to love. She continued to support him and understand what he must be going through. Preston spent most of his summer sitting on his rock at the Babbling Brook and she would watch him from afar. She noticed him looking around aimlessly, with no expression, making no sound. She wanted him to console in her and to seek her love. She knew he would come around one day, so she would watch him, wait and just be there by his side. She loved to look at him, his strong chin, his muscular body. She also loved, most of all, his mind but these days he only saw darkness and she had wondered what was going through his mind as he sat by the babbling brook. She could see the pain in his eyes. She would come closer. He knew that she was there, but he was almost unresponsive. She only wanted to ease his pain. She could see deep inside his soul, but it was like she didn't know this man and wondered how they would get through all of this. She hoped that he would find the light and know that this was not what Drew would have wanted, for them.

As summer drew closer to the end, the Hendersons and Banks sat around together for their last night in Haliburton. Preston had told them all that he would not be going back to school. When Annabelle tried to ask "why not," he gave her a dirty stare. He asked his father if he could join his company and Mr. Banks said "he couldn't be any happier to have a son by his side."

They left Haliburton separately, Annabelle with her parents and Preston with his. Annabelle waved to Preston and Preston only gave back an empty smile. Mrs. Henderson saw that her daughter was hurting, so she gave her some sound advice, reassuring her that one-day Preston would come back to her, like he had always done. She told her daughter she just needed to be understanding and give Preston as much space as he needed. He was not yet done grieving and he needed time, honey. You just need to be there for him.

Annabelle knew what her mother was saying was true. She was having a hard time, as she never thought Preston would shut her down the way he had. In her heart, she realized that Preston would have to deal with it in his own time. Annabelle started her third year at university, alone. Although it was strange that Preston was not near, she continued to excel in what she loved. She had become an excellent artist and spent most of her free time painting pictures of Preston and herself. She spent many lonely nights crying to herself. Preston barely called her and contacted her even less, personally. She wondered if Preston even thought of her. Was he still finding his way? It was hurting her that he felt he would rather be alone then to reach out to her. She wondered if he would move on without her. She knew deep down inside that she loved him and wanted to be near and help him.

Back at Bank's Pool and Hot Tubs, Mr. Banks was happy his son was there because one day this would all be Preston's. He wished Drew was still there, but he was happy that Preston was learning the business. He had seen in his son's face that he still was having hard times every day. He would give his son the time he needed, because, at that moment, he felt that he had lost both of his kids.

One night at dinner, Preston had finished his meal, thanked his mother and asked his father if he could have the keys to his Camaro. His father asked him "what's wrong son?" He said "dad I need a couple of days off." Mrs. Banks asked, "son are you alright?" Preston said "no mom, I just need some time to myself." She said "ok dear." and kindly reminded him that Annabelle had called every day. She was so worried as you don't return her calls and she wondered what she had done wrong. Preston replied, "mom, she has done nothing wrong, but right now my heart is empty. I just want to be alone. So, you tell her that if she needs to move on in her life, she can." Mrs. Banks felt as if her heart had fallen to her knees. She knew this his not Preston, but his heartbreak talking.

At this point Mrs. Banks knew that Preston wasn't himself. He was still not over his brother's death. Mr. Banks simply said nothing and gave his son the keys. Preston took the keys from his father along with his bag of clothes he had packed and threw the bag in the trunk of the Camaro. His parents were watching from the window and Mr. Banks said to Mrs. Banks, "he will be ok one day, he needs this time to grieve." Mrs. Banks asked "where do you think he is going? Mr. Banks said "I don't know." As Preston got into the car, he recalled he and his brother always arguing about who would get this car one day. Their father had bought the Camaro LS4 SS with 851 HP in

2016 and this was the first time Preston had ever driven it. He turned on the radio and the Gavin Degraw song "I don't want to be" was playing. It was Drew's favourite song. He drove as fast as he could. He was driving so fast, almost recklessly, with tears streaming down his face.

It was October and he had never been back to the cabin in Haliburton, where Preston and Drew had their greatest memories. As he got closer to the cabin, he stopped at Barney's Liquor Store and bought two bottles of bourbon. He thought it would make all his pain go away. He sat on the river bank, by his favourite place to be, as he consumed a bottle of bourbon. He waited for the wind to blow and although his judgement was blurred, he couldn't even hear the babbling brook which he thought odd, and he never heard one bird sing. He was weeping so hard that, when he wiped his tears, the salt was stinging his eyes. He had consumed the full bottle of bourbon and stumbled and fell many times on the way back to the cabin. Although he was heavily intoxicated, he had only been thinking about his brother and the pain he felt in his heart. He also knew that Annabelle was hurting but, at this point, he could only think of his brother. He climbed into bed, his clothes stained with mud. He went to sleep that night, with tears constantly flowing down his face. He remembered himself saying over and over, Drew. Drew. Drew. While he slept, he dreamt of his brother on the cliff. He was trying to run to his brother. To stop him. He couldn't get there fast enough and had woken up in a cold sweat. He knew it was a dream. He felt, once again, that if he could have been there he might have saved his brother's life. He whipped himself back to sleep.

The next morning, Mrs. Banks called Preston's phone repeatedly. He had not answered and the next minute she heard the doorbell ring. It was Annabelle frantically worried about Preston. Mrs. Banks asked Annabelle "what are you doing here? Shouldn't you be in school?" "I can't. All I think about is Preston. All I have ever done is love him, yet in the last four months he has barely spoken a word to me." Mrs. Banks feeling her pain, told Annabelle to come in and she would make them some tea. Annabelle obliged and sat down. At that point Mr. Banks came downstairs for breakfast. He could see that Annabelle had been crying, as her eyes were puffy and blood red. It had made him angry that his son could be so cruel, although he understood what Preston was feeling. He knew that Annabelle was there to help him and yet he had shut her out. Mrs. Banks and Mr. Banks consoled Annabelle and told her that one-day Preston would be back because they knew, deep down inside, he loved her. Mrs. Banks had asked Mr. Banks, if Preston had told him where he was. He needed to come home but Mr. Banks said to her "he needs his time." Mr. Banks could see the pain in Mrs. Banks and Annabelle's face. Mr. Banks had shared that he probably knew where his son had gone. Annabelle replied "where?" Mr. Banks said "I'm pretty sure he went to the cabin in Haliburton. I will finish my breakfast, get cleaned up and drive up there." Annabelle replied "I will come with you. I want to go there." Mr. Banks thought otherwise and shared with Annabelle that she should go back to school. He would go find Preston and then he would contact her to let her know that he was okay.

Although she was hesitant to agree, deep down inside she knew that Mr. Banks was right. Mr. Banks completed breakfast, got himself ready, gave his wife a kiss and said he would go get him. When

Mr. Banks got to the cabin, he knew he was right. His Camaro was there and to his relief the Camaro was in one piece. At first, Mr. Banks looked around. He searched the common spots that Preston and Drew would go, when he spotted Preston's shirt and a bottle of bourbon, his heart rate started to rise. He thought oh-my-God, don't tell me he jumped. He jumped in the stream and hoped that he would not find his son's body. After a few minutes of walking around in the cold frigid waters, he saw Preston coming to the brook. He stared at his father and asked with a smile "isn't it cold in there, dad?" With tears streaming down his eyes Mr. Banks told Preston that he would be grounded for the rest of his life. Mr. Banks came out of the water and they walked back to cabin and Preston threw on a pot of coffee to warm up his father. After Mr. Banks dried off and his clothes went in the dryer, he quickly called Mrs. Banks to let her know that Preston was okay and if she could please call Annabelle to let her know. Once the coffee was ready, Preston and his father sat at the table, like they had done so many times as a family. Mr. Banks understood Preston was dealing with his brother's loss and that he was there at his time of need. The rest of the day they sat around, and Preston told his father that he was sorry, that he knew he was adding to their stress, but its was just so hard for him to accept Drew would never be a part of their lives again. Mr. Banks simply replied "Preston, I understand what you are going through. It's been tough on me and your mother, Annabelle and the Hendersons. Remember Preston, this is not how Drew would want you to live. This is not how Drew would have ever lived his life so accept that you are having a hard time, but remember you are making it hard on all of us and we are grieving too." Preston had no reply. He knew his father was right.

At the end of the conversation Mr. Banks said "I'm here now, my pants are dry so let's go fishing." They spent the next few hours of that calm day, fishing the brooks and remembering all the fun times and memories of Drew. It was the first time in what seemed forever, that Preston had felt some joy. That night they had decided to stay, as it had gotten too late so, as they had done what they had done so many times before, they fried up the fish and Preston and his father sat by the fire drinking the rest of the bourbon, smiling, laughing and reflecting on all the great memories that he and his brother and their families had had. As they poured the last drink in the bottle, Preston asked his dad if it was ok if he took some time to himself and all Mr. Banks wanted to say to was that running away would not make his days any easier. But, understanding his son, he agreed.

The next morning, they drove home, and Preston told his mother his plans. His mother understood, although she was not happy. She only had one request, that he let Annabelle know. Preston obliged his mother and said "I will write a letter to explain what I am doing." So later that night, Preston wrote a letter, letting Annabelle know that he needed to take his own time and he was going away. He was going to travel. He needed to find his soul, once again. He didn't know when he would come back home, but he professed his love to her. He could never see himself loving anyone as much as he did her. He wanted her to move on with her life because he didn't feel that it was fair for him to hold her back. He assured her that nothing was her fault. He felt he needed to do this or he would never find true happiness for himself again. He said, in the end, he just didn't have enough love to love himself, let alone find enough love to share with someone else through this upside, down part of his life. I want you to find happiness. I fear, that if you wait for me, I may never find the peace in my heart anymore. You deserve a partnership of nothing less than beautiful harmony in your life. And then he packed, and was ready for bed because in the morning, he would be flying to Thailand.

CHAPTER 15

THAT MORNING PRESTON HAD awakened, jumped in his car and went to St. Josephs Cemetery, where his brother was resting in peace. He hadn't been back to see his brother in months. He sat there for an hour, just staring at the grave site. He felt a cold breeze on the back of his neck, as if he knew, Drew was there. He had explained to Drew that his life had seemed a loss. He explained that he felt responsible, that he should have been a better brother and, in that moment, another cold breeze circled him. The hairs on the back of Preston's neck stood up. He had investigated the sky and wondered how his brother was, if it is true that there was life after death.

He told him about what he was going to do, spending the next two years of his life teaching young children North American History and Mathematics. He was not going to be paid, as he was going to volunteer in honour of his brother's memory, Drew Banks. He felt that he needed time away to find himself, not with the luxuries that his fathers success had afforded him. He had told him about the letter he had written to Annabelle and as if Drew could understand, Preston had a shooting pain come across his body. It reminded him of all the words and passages that Drew would say, but his most favourite and famous was "Live life for today and make it so beautiful that it is worth remembering." He had told Drew how much he missed him, that he couldn't bear the thought of being at the cabin without him. He told him about the day he spent with their dad, drinking, fishing and remembering all the good times they shared. He hoped that one day he would come to grips with losing his brother, return and continue living for himself and for Drew. At that moment, he felt another cold breeze, as if Drew had understood and given his blessing. Preston kissed his brother's tombstone and said "I will see you later brother, when I come home." When Preston got home, his mother was sitting at the front door with his bags ready to go. He asked his mother "why are you crying?" As she wiped her tears back, she expressed to Preston she would not go to the airport with him and his dad. She had reminded him, fighting back her tears, "I can't bear to say goodbye to you right now. Please come home when you are ready Preston, I can't bear to lose another son." Preston reassured his mother he would be back and although his mother half believed him, she felt as if he had abandoned her in her time of need. Preston embraced his mother and explained "mom, I know it's hard for you, but I need to clear my head. I will be back one day and remember, I will never leave your side."

As Preston turned to leave he remembered he had written his letter to Annabelle and asked his mom not to give it to her for a few days. Mrs. Banks looked at her son and expressed her displeasure with the way he was leaving. He had been unfair to Annabelle, as all she wanted to do was love him. Instead he had built a wall between himself and her, almost as if to say, that it was Annabelle's fault that Drew made that jump. She closed the door when Preston left. She leaned against the door and she couldn't fight the feeling inside that when Drew died, Preston did as well. When Preston and his father got to the airport, Preston checked in and his father said simply, without a tear, "son do what you need to do, clear your head, find your peace, and do whatever it is necessary. Then come home to us no matter what, and remember that we love you." Mr. Banks sat and watched his son board the plane with tears streaming down his face. As Preston sat in his seat on the plane he too had tears in his eyes.

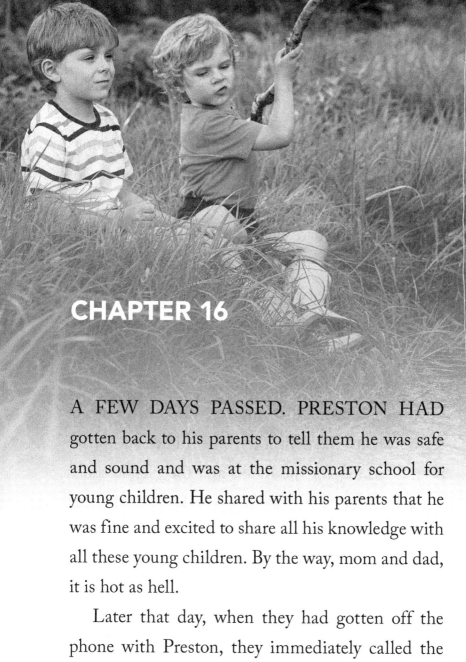

CHAPTER 16

A FEW DAYS PASSED. PRESTON HAD gotten back to his parents to tell them he was safe and sound and was at the missionary school for young children. He shared with his parents that he was fine and excited to share all his knowledge with all these young children. By the way, mom and dad, it is hot as hell.

Later that day, when they had gotten off the phone with Preston, they immediately called the Hendersons. They asked them if they could come over and the Hendersons replied "don't be silly. You are always welcome here." When the Banks arrived in Springwater they sat down at the table to enjoy some tea and refreshments and Mrs. Banks explained to the Hendersons that Preston had left, he had gone to Thailand to find himself and to educate young children. He felt it was something he wanted to do in honour of his brother. She told them that before Preston left, he had written a letter to Annabelle and Mrs. Banks wondered what she should do. Mrs. Henderson, being the class act that she was, understood that this was difficult for Elizabeth and Mr. Banks to deliver this news. They were worried and wondered how to approach Annabelle. Mr. Henderson reassured them they would drive up to the university and deliver the letter in person. It had been a sad day for the Banks and the Hendersons. They had hoped that Preston would find what he was looking for and that one day he would return to himself, and to Annabelle, and to all of them, but for now they would have to accept and respect Preston's decisions and choices. The next few hours were spent together as they had always done, enjoying each others company and the Banks apologized for their son's actions and choices. The Hendersons simply said "these are hurdles that we must meet and jump".

As the Banks drove back to Midhurst, Mr. and Mrs. Henderson got in their car and drove to see their daughter.

When they had got to Annabelle's dorm, her roommate said she had not returned but to come in, she should be here soon. When Annabelle arrived, she was surprised and happy to see her parents. Although, it was strange for them to visit on week days, she could not have known what was coming next. Mrs. Henderson handed Preston's letter to Annabelle, and that she thought Annabelle needed to sit, so she sat at the edge of the bed with Mrs. Henderson by her side. As Annabelle read the letter, her eyes welled up, her tears turned to streams and her mother and father could feel her pain. When she was done reading all the letter, she stayed seated on the bed beside her mother for what seemed like a lifetime, with a blank stare. Mr. Henderson had no words and then Annabelle said "What did I do? All I ever did was love Preston. I loved Drew. I just wanted to help him. He shut me out. He made me feel as if he didn't want me around and now he writes me this letter, telling me I should move on, I shouldn't worry and that he loves me. How could he leave me without a goodbye kiss, saying he didn't want me to contact him, that it was best I find someone else? How would he expect me to take this mom, tell me how should I feel?" "Well, honey, I don't know how you should feel. I know you are hurt and I know those words were hard to take, but let's try to understand how Preston feels." "Well, I am done trying to understand how Preston feels. How about how I feel? I feel betrayed and my only mistake was loving him so much. My reward is that he spits in my face." Mr. Henderson was completely uncomfortable. He felt like a fish out of water. He understood his daughter and how she felt, but he also understood how difficult it must be for Preston. How hard it must have been to write the girl you love, feeling the pain of letting her go and right now it must be a hard place for Preston to be in. The Hendersons asked their daughter if she wanted to come home and she explained to her parents that she would be alright. She needed time to understand her feelings now and that she needed her space. School was the best place to be right now. The Hendersons left their daughter to process what happened, Mrs. Henderson wondering how it was possible that their love could have changed, but it was not for her to judge or understand. She would respect her daughter's wishes and only time would tell, if her heart once again, would be filled with love.

As Annabelle laid down to sleep, she had wondered what had gone so wrong. She knew, in her heart, she would never stop loving Preston or see herself with another man. He had always been and would always be, the love of her life. That night she remembered how wonderful their love was and she hoped that one day her lover, her friend, Preston, would come back to her. Until then, she would continue living life, like she knew Drew would want. She wondered, if Preston never came back to her, would he find the arms of other women and that moment she wished he was there, so she could knock some sense into his head, but then kiss his head better. She closed her eyes and prayed that her Preston would be safe and return to her one day.

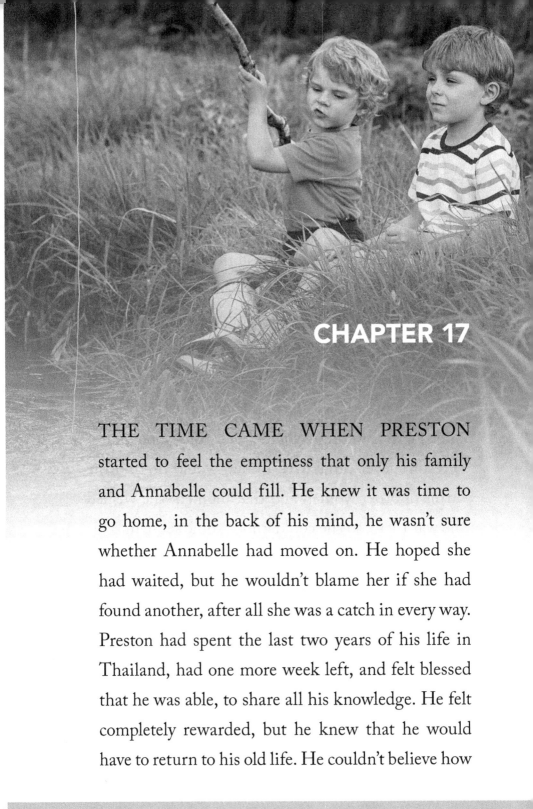

CHAPTER 17

THE TIME CAME WHEN PRESTON started to feel the emptiness that only his family and Annabelle could fill. He knew it was time to go home, in the back of his mind, he wasn't sure whether Annabelle had moved on. He hoped she had waited, but he wouldn't blame her if she had found another, after all she was a catch in every way. Preston had spent the last two years of his life in Thailand, had one more week left, and felt blessed that he was able, to share all his knowledge. He felt completely rewarded, but he knew that he would have to return to his old life. He couldn't believe how much he had missed Annabelle and his parents. The last two years had also been tough on the Banks and they felt very alone. They had spent most of their time with the Hendersons and Annabelle and they could see Annabelle was missing Preston deeply. They hadn't really, brought up Preston's name. They had all enjoyed the summers at the cabin together, although it had seemed very lonely and quiet at night.

They had noticed Annabelle's paintings and how incredibly beautiful they were. She had graduated university with high honours and started her new job as director of the Museum of Fine Arts in Alcona and her parents couldn't have been any prouder. Annabelle had always been dear to them, but over the last few years they had grown to admire her courage, her talents, and most of all the respect that she had for everyone else. They had noticed she was the kind of person who could go into a dark room and bring sunshine to everyone. Although, Annabelle never talked about Preston and rarely spoke of Drew, Mrs. Banks knew that Annabelle was always thinking of Preston. When she had painted, for her thesis, a work of art, it was a picture of Preston and Drew sitting at the babbling brook and had simply called the art,

"The Love of Two Brothers." Through that painting, Mrs. Banks had understood that Annabelle had never stopped loving Preston and she had wondered if Preston still loved Annabelle. She hoped so, because she couldn't bear the thought of any other woman being her daughter-in-law. Annabelle had many suitors and had not only heard it from her mother, many times, while they were having lunch with Mrs. Banks, but she had seen how men glanced at her ruby red lips, spectacular blue eyes and the body of a Greek goddess. It seemed that Annabelle was unaware, or simply had not cared.

Although Mrs. Banks herself continued to encourage Annabelle to live her life and forget about Preston, Annabelle had reassured Mrs. Banks that her true love would one day come back to her. Although, Mrs. Banks had her doubts at times, she had hoped her son would see the light. Annabelle had loved her new job and it had been her dream to one day be a curator of a museum or art gallery. She had finished graduating, applied to a few places, and all of them expressed their pleasure to have her as leader of the staff. Her talents as an artist showed her pure love and appreciation of all art forms. Her passion for art at every level, was magical, and contagious. This pure love of art showed through in every one of her interviews. I suppose it was this that made Preston and anyone that encountered her, to be so enthralled and amazed by the energy this woman could bring. Yet some days Annabelle could not understand how the man that she loved more than anyone in this world, could cut her off like she didn't exist, but being a strong and independent woman, she continued to enjoy life. Her heart was filled with emptiness, waiting and hoping that Preston would return. But, doubt had set in, it had been over two years, since she had heard a whisper from Preston.

CHAPTER 18

PRESTON HAD SPENT THE LAST TWO years, at best a shadow, in the accommodations provided by the school. Preston was used to a life of luxury, in Thailand just having a washroom was luxury. To Preston it didn't matter, he believed this was a good lesson, he appreciated more what he had in life. Meals consisted of mostly rice and root vegetables with fish as a staple. Once every month or so, he would appreciate the taste of chicken or goat, unlike his life back in Midhurst, with his family, where there was always steak and hamburgers. He had grown to appreciate the simple things in life, he thought to himself. He would miss the smiling faces of the children that attended class.

He had realized, to himself, how much he had taken for granted in the privileged life he had been fortunate to live. Simple things, like the two-ply toilet paper he had been accustomed to in Midhurst. The one he used now was the equivalent of cardboard boxes. But the children were so rewarded with simple things, like knowledge, because for most of these children life was fishing, harvesting vegetables and simply living as a family, blessed just to have food on the table and clothes on their backs. Those simple things, like just having a roof made of straw over your head and a pair of sandals that kept their feet safe while walking on bare ground. When he had first got to Thailand he had realized that not only air conditioning, but simple things like having enough food to feed your family and clean drinking water for your family, was an accomplishment that most were not able to provide. Yet, these people still managed to smile, and rejoice in simple things like the first major rainstorm. It had lasted about three days into the trip, the rainfall had brought so much joy to boys and girls. They would run in it as if they had received a gift and for Preston, that was incredible. He had often thought if, when Drew and himself had been little boys, had they found contentment in something as simple as rain. The treehouse that their father had built in Haliburton, filled with toys, was more than any of these children would ever have or even knew existed in their world.

When he had free time, he had often wondered what his parents were doing. What Annabelle was doing. He had longed for a taste of steak and knew that he had lived a luxurious life. He had seen the faces of children suffering from malnutrition, that simple things like clean drinking water was considered a luxury. It had shown him that he had been blessed, that like himself, these children had not chosen their life. They had not been shown any other life, but simply the love of parents and family is worth a million pounds in gold. He was now ready to go home and pick up the pieces that he had left behind. He hoped that Annabelle was still there, waiting for him and that his mother and father could forgive him for being so selfish and abandoning them in what must have been the hardest time of their life. He hoped that his brother was not looking down at him with disgust. He had felt he was the only person that could possibly feel the way he felt, by losing his brother.

Preston, at that point, could not see the light from the darkness in his mind. He had one more week left in Thailand and couldn't wait to get home to see his mother and father, but most of all Annabelle. This week he was rejoicing and feeling great about how he had come through this darkness, the joy that he had brought to all the young girls and boys of Thailand, and the feeling he had received from every one of these strangers made him feel truly blessed. He could not have been more thankful that he had experienced these last two years. It had brought him happiness, humility and an education of what truly matters in life. He realized that no matter what happened in your life, you must carry on for the loved ones who have passed and the loved ones who were there to love and support you. You must not forget to be humble and return your love and support to the ones that loved you.

He had been lying in bed when he recalled the past few months. He was thinking back to his brothers past, and the ones that he had isolated and abandoned, all of whom had loved him. He remembered coming to a winding road and at the end of the road there was a temple. He had gone into the temple and was amazed with the silence. All the people were praying. He had realized he needed to look deep inside himself and ask for forgiveness, guidance and the strength to repair what he had hurt in his life. When he was done, he recalled walking outside. There was an old man standing there, with a long white beard and long silky hair. He was holding an old walking stick, that looked like it was made of bamboo. He put his hand on Preston's shoulder and said to him in broken English, "you walk with all the weight of the world on your shoulders son." He continued asking him a few questions. He asked "Did you go into the temple to pray?." and Preston replied "yes." "What did you ask god?" Preston thought about what he had prayed for. "Did he answer your question?" Preston smiled and had thought it was peculiar, that this old man would ask such a question. Then, he had continued and the old man spoke once again. He said "he did not answer your question, but pray he will show you the way and when it is time, your time, you will find peace. Ask the lord to give you peace and salvation, you will then find your peace." Preston had looked at the old man and said "my brother is dead." With the butt end of his cane he had tapped Preston on the forehead and said "yes my boy, but use your brain, your brother is dead but he lives on, when you are happy, he lives on when you rejoice, but when you are sad and walk around aimlessly, you tarnish all that he lived for and that is not what he wants you to do."

Your brother, his life is everlasting, you live through him and when it is your time, he will call and you will go. You will live life on Earth the best way you can. You will go when God is ready to accept us to live with him, but you must live today and every day, for yourself, the way your brother would have lived for you. Your brother has gone to heaven. One day you will go too, with the saviour and you will see your brother again," and with that he had thanked the old man who had helped him find peace.

Now, looking back, If, it had been Drew losing Preston, he would have been sad that he had lost him, but he would have lived and made both of their lives proud. In that moment, Preston could hardly wait to get back and live his life, for himself and his brother. He would ask forgiveness from Anabelle, his parents and the Hendersons, for he had found the strength. He would devote the rest of his life, living it to the fullest, sharing happiness with all. This is how he would honour his brother Drew and Preston had woken up. When It had been time to go, he had thanked all the boys and girls, the headmaster and Mr. Yoshi. Before he left for the airport, he had sought out the old man once more and when he got to the temple he had asked the monk "Where is the old man with the cane, long grey beard and silky grey hair. They called him, Massyoti. The monk looked at him, puzzled, and said "sorry, but Massyoti has been dead for ten years." Preston said "I had just spoken with him couple of months ago." Again the monk responded and had said "son, that was not possible." At that point, Preston knew that heaven did exist.

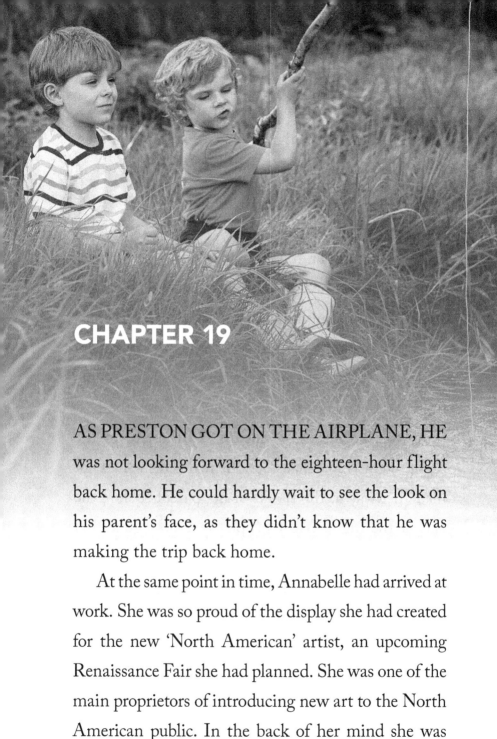

CHAPTER 19

AS PRESTON GOT ON THE AIRPLANE, HE was not looking forward to the eighteen-hour flight back home. He could hardly wait to see the look on his parent's face, as they didn't know that he was making the trip back home.

At the same point in time, Annabelle had arrived at work. She was so proud of the display she had created for the new 'North American' artist, an upcoming Renaissance Fair she had planned. She was one of the main proprietors of introducing new art to the North American public. In the back of her mind she was excited and proud of herself, but she wished Preston was here to see it. She had no idea when Preston would be coming home and kept busy setting up her displays. Annabelle made sure that everyone was on their toes, because she knew at this Renaissance Fair, there would be artists, critics and art enthusiasts from all over the world. She knew her parents and the Banks would be there to support her. It was a busy day, filled with tons of people, art enthusiasts and professionals, alike. She received many congratulations from people, teachers and old friends, had conducted many interviews and smiled through them all. Even though it had become tiresome, she was a pro and knew this was the best thing for the Alcona Museum. By the end of the night, she was so exhausted. She realized she had not made her way to the Banks or her parents before the end of the night. Most people were now gone, but her parents and the Banks had hung around to the very end. She finally got to speak her parents, who had smiles from ear to ear. They couldn't have been prouder of their daughter. The Banks were also very proud of Annabelle because they had always looked at her like a daughter. They knew she would be a successful. By the end of the night, they were all tired and she thanked them all for coming, apologizing for not giving them more of her time. They knew she was busy. It was her time to shine and they didn't mind at all. They couldn't have been happier. They hadn't seen Annabelle this happy since before Drew passed.

As the Banks were driving home, Mrs. Banks said "I am so proud of Annabelle, but I wish that Preston was here for her." Mr. Banks agreed. Meanwhile Preston was still only half way home. Preston had had a few cocktails. He was feeling good, at this point, and he realized he would soon be home, hoping no one had forgotten about him. Although he had been a horses' ass for the last few years, he was still excited and was looking forward to seeing everyone. He hoped he could rejoin his father and maybe, one day, take over ownership of Bank's Pools and Hot Tubs.

During the next few hours, Preston fell asleep and when he awoke, the plane had touched down in Midhurst. He went through customs and was thinking what he would say, when he first saw his mother and father. He was thinking about what they would think about their son, wondering if it was possible that Annabella was still in love with him, thinking that, if she wasn't, he couldn't blame her.

As he came out of the airport, he took a taxi. It was early in the morning, He was determined to get home for he was truly homesick, and as they turned the corner he was home, and it felt great. Mr. and Mrs. Banks were sitting at the table. They could see the driveway from the kitchen table when suddenly, an orange taxi pulled up the driveway. Mrs. Banks noticed the taxi first, looked at her husband and said "are you expecting someone?" At that point the trunk of the taxi opened, the door opened, and there was their son, Preston, standing on the driveway. The taxi drove off, Mr. Banks noticed the ghost of the boy he knew. It was his son, back home with them. His eyes welled up, full of tears. "Is that you Preston?" His father ran out the door and his mom right behind him. They all embraced as they had never done before. Preston's eyes and his parent's eyes welled up many times over the past few years, but this time, it was joy, pure joy. Preston looked at his parents and said "I'm home, home for good, ready to be your son." And Mr. Banks said "you never stopped being our son. We're just glad you're home." Preston said "so am I, it's been too long."

CHAPTER 20

AS THE BANKS MADE THEIR WAY BACK inside the house, Mr. Banks looked up to God and said "thank you for bringing my son home." And as always, they sat at the table, Mrs. Banks putting on a pot of tea and Preston smiled knowing he was home and it felt great. He began to tell his parents all about his travels, about the wonderful children that he taught, and how their appreciation of life was different than those in North America. They had opened his eyes and saw what was important in life and despite being thankful for the life his parents have given him, he now understood, what true life is about. These people, who have very little in the way of material things, were thankful for the simple things. Things were not taken for granted, like clean drinking water and simple food made of rice and vegetables, to feed their families. Things like running water or an inside toilet were considered a luxury and only rich people could afford a toilet and indoor plumbing. Many students of his, came to school with holes in their shoes and rips in their clothing, but hey were happy just to be attending school. Going to school provided them with the skills that would help them in later life. He would always remember the smiles of knowledge on their face and that rewarded him greater than anything he had accomplished in his life or would for the rest of his life. He told them about the first few days, about the children playing in the rain, and the joy it brought was contagious. He remembered himself engaged in running in the rain and feeling the warmth, how he felt so welcomed and loved by complete strangers, spending many days and nights invited to these people's homes. They would share their food, even though they had very little, yet these people could enjoy family life as if they were the richest people in the world, even though they had come from a background of simple means.

It humbled Preston to think that he could be so selfish, hurting all the people around him, his family and loved ones. It brought perspective not only in the way Preston viewed them, but the way he viewed myself. Preston had spent many nights in the past few years, self-loathing, and it had been a complete embarrassment to look in the mirror. It was hard to look at, to see all the sorrow that he had caused his family and Annabelle. He felt as if his brother Drew was looking down on him with distain. If Drew would have been me and I would have been Drew, he would have carried a heavy heart, but he would have continued to live and not make the bad choices I made. The people of Thailand had taught him what he should have already known. What Preston remembered was that saying, from Drew's lips. Even though he was a trouble maker and a pest, his words ring true every day and through those words, live life for today, making every day worth remembering, he would live a more complete and full life. Mr. and Mrs. Banks looked at each other puzzled by their son. They couldn't believe that this was their Preston, so quiet, so afraid to show emotion, to tell anyone how he felt. They were so proud that even though they had missed him, he had come back a better man. They continued listening to what Preston had to say, sharing all the enlightenment his brother had said, live for today, as it's for remembering!

Preston had gone to Thailand to teach, but, in truth, he had become the student. Having seen how people live, in the world, his fondest memories were sitting around their dinner table. They treated me like I was royalty, simply because I was there educating their children and asking for nothing in return. I realized as I looked around at each table I sat at, that while these people deal with everyday life that was a struggle, they found a way, in their souls, to find true happiness. I mean true happiness, just sitting around, knowing they had their family. I even saw one family lose their child to malnutrition and I remember how their older brother would just stare and stare at me. He would say "I am so blessed, to have had my brother and to know him for the short time that I did. One day, I want to write a book of how wonderful my brother was." It was at that point, Preston realized that he was lucky enough to have lived eighteen years with the most dynamic loving brother, he could have had. The Banks just stared at their son and asked nothing. When Preston had gone up to bed, because he was exhausted, Mr. Banks simply said to Mrs. Banks, "wow, he really has found happiness and I hope that he will find his way back into the heart of Annabelle. It's been a long journey, an uphill battle that Preston fought with his inner demons." Mr. Banks remembered every time the doorbell rang, the look that appeared on Elizabeth's face, could see the worried look that one day it would be somebody saying that our son had passed as well. To lose one son or daughter is heart wrenching, but two, tests every morale fibre of your belief in God and life, but through God's wisdom and our love, Preston had found his way back in to their hearts and home. Mr. Banks only hope was that Preston was content enough, and live a long, prosperous life. That night, for the first time in a few years, Mrs. Banks and Mr. Banks holding each other tightly, fell asleep with the happiness that their son was safely home.

CHAPTER 21

THE NEXT MORNING, ANNABELLE WAS
sitting at the table with her parents. Her father had
gone outside to get the Springwater newspaper. With
a big smile on his face, he came back into the kitchen
and Annabelle asked her father "what you are smiling
about?" Her father replied "oh nothing, just that I
have the best daughter in the world". Mrs. Henderson
was smiling and wondered what her husband had
meant. "Simply dear, our daughter is on the front
page of the Springwater News. Her Renaissance
Fair was an absolute smash, and the CEO of the
Alcona Museum, Mr. Trout had given all the credit

to Ms. Annabelle Henderson, saying he couldn't have been prouder to have brought Annabelle to the Alcona Museum." He goes on to say "since she has been here, she has brought success, not only to the museum, but to the town of Alcona and for the first time in fifteen years, the Alcona museum will turn a profit. Mr. Trout went on to say that Annabelle's understanding of modern art, and that alone, was creating a buzz for her recognition of the artists in North America as well as her appointed staff." Mr. Henderson read on and Annabelle blushed.

Her mother could not have been any prouder, but Annabelle reminded her parents it takes more than one person to recognize and make a business a success. She simply looked at her father and said "you, know that dad. Henderson Motors takes a great staff and a lot of hard work." Mrs. Henderson couldn't be prouder of her daughter. Annabelle reminded everyone that she didn't take the job because she needed the recognition, she simply loved what she did. She was aware of the talented artists, sculptors and painters that we have in North America and was only there to protect, harvest the art, and care for the museum's artifacts. It was nice to be recognized but it was not a big deal. Mr. Henderson didn't feel that way. He didn't mind letting everyone know about his wonderful daughter. Annabelle simply replied to her father," oh, dad." That night Mr. Trout had planned a party for all the staff at the museum and the local newspapers. Annabelle was not in the mood to party but she felt it her obligation, as team leader, to be there. It was at their local pub in Alcona, The Grasshopper Eatery. They had rented out the facility for the night and although it had been a wonderful evening, Annabelle was ready for sleep.

There was one young man that worked at the Alcona Museum, that had a thing for Annabelle. All the other ladies that worked at the Alcona Museum knew that Nick Shultz had the hots for Annabelle, but it did not matter to Annabelle, because dating was not even close to her radar. After a few drinks, Nick decided that he would approach Annabelle.

He simply asked her if she would entertain going out for dinner or a movie, with him. Annabelle said "there is only one man that holds my heart and if it takes the rest of my life for him to realize it, I will be waiting. She was fine with that." Nick put his tail between his legs and hit on the next girl. Annabelle thanked Mr. Trout, all the guests and the members of her team that had made the Renaissance Fair such a success, that she looked forward to the next one. Annabelle, being tired, went home.

The next morning Preston awoke to the fresh smell of coffee, knew that he was home again and that he had a few things to do. First, was to ask his father, if he could once again work for his dad's company. With a split-second decision, his father said "you don't know how long, I have waited for you to say that. I can't believe this day has come. I had my doubts. I want you to learn everything because it is a family business and one day it will yours." Mr. and Mrs. Banks could not have been happier. Preston then asked his father if he could wait one more week, because he wanted to spend some time alone in Haliburton. He explained to his mother and father that if they could please respect his wishes, not letting the Hendersons or Annabelle catch wind that he was home, he would be grateful. Mrs. Banks asked "but why son, don't you think she has suffered enough?" Preston answered "yes mother."

He knew how much he put her through but Preston wanted to write her a letter and had not had time to write one. Preston was going to write the letter, wait a few days and then have it mailed to the Henderson's house in Springwater. If Annabelle wants me then she will know where to find me. Preston needed some time in Haliburton, to make his peace. "But you have never stayed up there in November," Mrs. Banks replied. Mr. Banks told his wife "I haven't closed the cabin yet" and Preston smiled, looked at his dad and asked "why not? Mr. Banks said "I'm not as young, as I used to be." Preston explained that by spending a week at the cabin, by himself, he felt that he would be ready to start a new life, a happier life a more fulfilled life. If Preston was going to spend the rest of his life with Annabelle, he would be better prepared, and if not, he would be prepared for that outcome as well as had made things the way they are.

So, Preston packed up a few things, gave his mother and father a peck on their cheeks and started his journey to Haliburton. He thought of Haliburton almost every day when he was in Thailand. He missed the sounds of the birds, the calmness of the babbling brook, the beautiful lake, and the cool air of the nights. He had never experienced the coldness of a November night, but felt that if he spent some time up there, he would know the right words to say to Annabelle, that is, if she could find it in her heart to forgive, the pompous ass he had been. He was almost in the hills of Halliburton when he noticed it had started to snow, and he could not recall it being so beautiful as it was right now. He arrived at the cabin tears, streaming down his face, and before he even moved a bag, he walked to the babbling brook. Everything was covered with a fine blanket of snow. He had never seen it look so beautiful. The echoes of the babbling brook, the waters had never been so crystal clear he could see a light film of ice, cascading over the water. He couldn't remember the place he loved looking more beautiful, than it did now. He wished Drew was here, but he knew that would never happen again. He was now ready. He knew what he would write in the letter to the woman of his dreams, the one he left behind, the love of his life, his soulmate Annabelle Henderson.

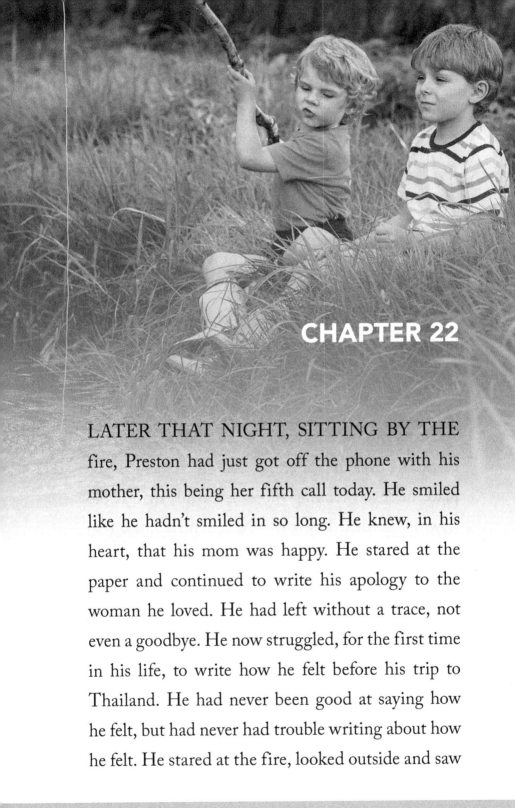

CHAPTER 22

LATER THAT NIGHT, SITTING BY THE fire, Preston had just got off the phone with his mother, this being her fifth call today. He smiled like he hadn't smiled in so long. He knew, in his heart, that his mom was happy. He stared at the paper and continued to write his apology to the woman he loved. He had left without a trace, not even a goodbye. He now struggled, for the first time in his life, to write how he felt before his trip to Thailand. He had never been good at saying how he felt, but had never had trouble writing about how he felt. He stared at the fire, looked outside and saw how beautiful the light snow was. He had wondered many times during the night, why they had never come to the cabin in the woods to see the true beauty of the fall or the winter.

This was the way he now saw many things in life, they were clear. Through the love for simply things, and his new appreciation for life, he had finally found the inspiration to explain and to apologize, in hopes that Annabelle still loved him. He wrote a very simple letter, explaining that his life without her would be an endless road to nowhere. He would be just a lost soul, how he felt like he had walked through fire, his thoughts of her had kept his body safe. The thought of his last breath, without her by his side, would be heart- breaking. He said he would understand if she never wanted to see him again. How he probably didn't deserve her, even though he had been so far away in distance, in his heart he had never stopped loving her. His mother had explained how Annabelle's career and her dream job had transpired. He wished that he could have been there to support her, like she had always been there for him.

That night, he fell asleep in the rocking chair, in front of the fire. He had a sense of warmness and wellness, as he slept he dreamt of his brother Drew. Drew's message was simple. I know you felt the pain of losing me and I wish that I had been more like you and less like me. I want you to be happy and to know that I am happy. You are sad and you have caused so much pain to Annabelle. I want you to live, so I need you to remember that you need to "live for today, and make it so beautiful, that it is worth remembering," I will send you a sign one day, one day soon, and you will know that it is me. I hope that you will find happiness in your life. I wish the best for you and don't forget to love Annabelle the way you love me. Suddenly, Preston woke up, and with the words from his brother, completed his letter and without going back to bed mailed it to Annabelle. The next time Preston woke it had snowed during the whole night. There was at least six inches of fresh snow on the ground and when Preston had made himself a cup of coffee, he took the mug and walked out to the babbling brook. He noticed the brook was icy, still and beautiful. He had so many fond memories of all the time he had spent there, was so grateful that he had that time with his brother and Annabelle, and he realized most people don't get this chance at life, love, or friendship. He could only hope Annabelle could find it in her heart to forgive and love him again. They hoped they could renew the friendship and the love that they had shared in their youth and young adulthood.

He knew that the sunshine that was breaking through the clouds on this day, on the water of the babbling brook, was the sign. It was time to forgive, to ask to be forgiven and to carry on the memory of not only, his love for Annabelle, but also the love of his brother. He would cherish all the time they had had together. He hoped that Annabelle would come and they would live their life as he had always wanted to.

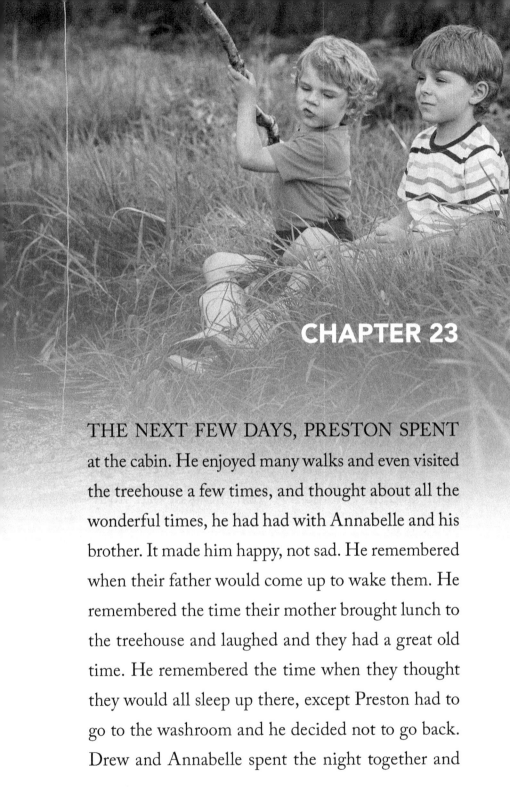

CHAPTER 23

THE NEXT FEW DAYS, PRESTON SPENT at the cabin. He enjoyed many walks and even visited the treehouse a few times, and thought about all the wonderful times, he had had with Annabelle and his brother. It made him happy, not sad. He remembered when their father would come up to wake them. He remembered the time their mother brought lunch to the treehouse and laughed and they had a great old time. He remembered the time when they thought they would all sleep up there, except Preston had to go to the washroom and he decided not to go back. Drew and Annabelle spent the night together and the next day teased him, saying he was such a suck. He remembered how beautiful Annabelle was as a young girl. He knew, that she knew, how he felt but he could never find the courage or words to tell her. He knew, deep down inside, Annabelle had felt the same. They had a special relationship, she was the Ying to his Yang. He spent many days hiking and loved the sound of the snow crushing under his feet. Many times, he wondered why they had never come up to the cabin in the winter. It had been a few days since he sent the letter and wondered if it had been lost or did Annabelle tear it up? He hoped that she would find it in her heart to forgive him, but if she didn't, he would know why. He started a fire that night and sat beside it, pouring himself a bourbon. Before long, he had fallen asleep, once again by the fire.

The next day, Mrs. Henderson had gotten a knock at the door, noticed it was the mailman. He said "good morning Mrs. Henderson. I have a letter for you and you must sign for it." She said thank you and it was, at that moment, that she had noticed the letter was for Annabelle from Preston. She called Mrs. Banks. "I just received a letter from

Preston. Is he alright?" "Yes," answered Mrs. Banks. "Why didn't you tell us he was back?" "He swore me to secrecy. He needed to go away for couple more days to find the right words to say to Annabelle." Mrs. Henderson, being the kind soul she was, had just simply asked "is it a letter to break her heart further?" Mrs. Banks replied "I don't know what he has written, but I know he missed her dearly." With that, Mary simply ran upstairs, called her husband and explained the letter. He said "I hope it's not a bad letter." "I talked to Elizabeth and Preston had gone up to the cottage to find the words to write how sorry he was." "You're damn right. He should be sorry," and Mary answered "keep your opinions to yourself." Mr. Henderson said," I just don't want to see Annabelle get hurt more." Mrs. Henderson responded to her husband, "I recall a time when you weren't such a great man either" and with that Mr. Henderson looked down, saying no more. When he felt, it was safe to open his mouth, he asked his wife what the plan was.

She said "I'm going to drive over to the museum and hand the letter to Annabelle myself." Mr. Henderson said "alright dear, let me know if there are any problems." Mary got dressed, brushed her teeth, left the curlers in her hair and with no makeup, ran out the door. She couldn't believe all the traffic lights were turning red and of course it always happened when you are in a hurry. As she bobbed and weaved through traffic, her heart was pounding with excitement, or fear, she had not yet known which. When she arrived at the museum, she barely got her seatbelt off and ran into the museum. She spotted Annabelle who said "mom you still have curlers in your hair and no makeup." Mrs. Henderson replied "never mind that dear. I have a surprise for you." Annabelle said "what is it mom?" "It's a letter." Why had her mother come here, first thing in the morning? Annabelle noticed it was not any old letter, it was from Preston, her hand started to tremble. She could barely get the words out and asked her mother "what does it say?" and her mother replied "I haven't opened it, dear." Annabelle thought to herself, well, mom, come on, let's open it. She wondered if he had finally written her to let her know he was not coming back? The fear that hit her was overwhelming. She thought that the letter meant he doesn't love me and doesn't want me in his life. She could hardly wait to read it, but the tears were streaming down her face too strongly. She asked her mother "could you please read me what it says" Her mother replied "are you sure you want me to read what he has written?" Annabelle replied "yes mother, I think it's best." So, Mrs. Henderson started to read. "My Dearest Annabelle, I know it has been a long time. I left without notice. I left without even telling you how I felt. When I left, my heart was aching, my mind unclear. The pain was too deep. I couldn't see the light through the darkness. If you hate me, I will understand. I hope you can forgive me, I know I have caused you great pain and for that, I am so sorry. I was lost, but now I am found. I have lived, but without you, I have not lived. I once loved and I hope to love again but without you I am not alive. I hope if you still have any love in your heart for me, I believe you know where to find me. Always yours. Love Preston." Mrs. Henderson stared at her daughter and for a moment Annabelle, for probably first time in life, was at a loss for words.

Her mother asked "Do you need to sit down dear?" "No mom, I need to go to Preston. I know where he is." As they rushed out of the museum, she simply told the secretary she would be back tomorrow or would call. They rushed to the car and Mrs. Henderson asked "Where are we going?" " To Haliburton mom. That's where Preston is waiting for me, I'm sure of it". As Mrs. Henderson, floored it, all the way to Haliburton Annabelle was crying and for no reason, her mother joined in too. Annabelle looked at her mother and asked "why you are crying?" "I'm crying with happiness," and her mom just smiled back at her. Annabelle knew that her man had come back to her. Preston would be waiting at the cabin in Haliburton. As Mrs. Henderson came to a stop, Annabelle flew out of the car, running into the house, but Preston wasn't upstairs or anywhere to be found. She felt her heart pounding. She found herself running to the treehouse. Her mother could barely keep up, but Preston wasn't there either. She had wondered where he was, then she thought how could she be so foolish. He would be sitting at the babbling brook.

As she came close, she spotted Preston. He looked much thinner. He had a beard for the first time ever. My God, she thought, he was very handsome. She slowed her heart beat and stared down at Preston for a few seconds. She wanted to run into his arms and then she thought about punching him, but she loved him and she didn't want to bruise his face. Mrs. Henderson yelled out Preston's name. He turned around and was face to face with the woman he loved. Annabelle could barely contain herself. She rushed into Preston's arms and kissed him all over. At that moment, they both burst into tears, and Mrs. Henderson could not control her emotions. Annabelle said to Preston "I have missed you so much, every night my heart ached for you." And Preston replied, "I'm sorry, I ached for you as well." They embraced and continued to kiss each other with such passion and vigor. He held her tight as they looked upon the babbling brook. It was like they were caught up in the moment, back in each other's arms and to Mrs. Henderson it was the most beautiful scene she had ever witnessed. She knew that from that moment, her daughter's heart was going to heal. Mrs. Henderson stayed, where she was. As they hugged, it was like something around them was happening, out of nowhere, a cold windy breeze made the hair on Preston and Annabelle's skin stand up, and even the few birds that were still there, were singing a tune they had never heard before. The melody the babbling brook had played was so sweet and at that moment, Preston knew that Drew was there. Preston looked at Annabelle and said "I'm cold, I need a cup of tea. Would you like one too?" Mrs. Henderson, at this point, could not stand by anymore, she needed to join them.

She was so lost in the moment with them that felt that she herself was a young girl once again. She could see such love between her daughter and Preston, she also embraced him, like the son she had lost. She gave her daughter a kiss on the head and one for Preston too. She told Preston and Annabelle "I think you have some catching up to do, could you bring her home?" Preston had assured her that he would and thanked her for being there for him, like his parents. He was so sorry for hurting her daughter and as always Mrs. Henderson knew what to say "I know you're a good man and sometimes it just takes a man to remember that he has a good woman waiting for him." Without any more said, Mrs., Henderson got into the car and pulled away.

Annabelle and Preston waved goodbye. They went inside, Annabelle putting on the kettle for tea. Preston lit a fire, he couldn't believe how beautiful she was. It had only been a few years, but it has seemed like forever. The fire was roaring and the tea was warm. They sat by the fire, Preston staring into her beautiful eyes. He couldn't believe that he had ever left her and wasn't by her side. That night the winds were howling and if you listened closely, you could even hear the wolves howl. In that moment, Annabelle grabbed Preston tight with all her might. She wasn't the shy girl he left, she knew what she wanted and needed, so she made her feelings felt. He caressed her beautiful long hair, it had felt like silk. Her eyes were like blue sapphires, her skin like cashmere. He ran his fingertip across her lips, he caressed her like he had never done before. He slowly moved his lips and kissed her soft skin. She could feel his warmth and passion. She had hungered for him for so long, for the smell of passion. He took her in his arms like a savage, she couldn't believe that this was her Preston, but not that she was complaining. She felt his warmth inside her. It was a night that she had hoped for, longing for Preston to be with her. He made love to her like only a princess could dream. Her prince had come to her again, tonight would be the start of their unbridled passion, like it had never been before. She had dreamed of this day for the last few years, hoping, waiting, wooing him back. Now that he was there, she could not have dreamed a night like this, filled with love and compassion, not even from her dear sweet Preston. They spent the rest of the night making love in front of the fire.

The next morning, Preston awoke with Annabelle beside him and without a whisper, he got up, made breakfast and put on a pot of coffee. Annabelle woke to the sweet aromas of love. She put on Preston's pants and covered herself with a blanket, then sat down at the table to the meal that this hunk of a man, the love of her life, had made. As they ate breakfast, they both stared at each other with affectionate smiles. They cleaned up. As they were getting ready, Preston, the bashful man she once knew, had other ideas before going back home. He picked her up and once again carried her to the front of the fire and took her with lust and unbridled passion. She wasn't sure who he was anymore, but she was loving how much of an animal this new man was, and she was wet from all his loving. She had only dreamed that this sweet man she loved could make all her erotic dreams come true. When they had finished, she had tried to get ready to go, but he was an animal and she wasn't able, to resist him once more. When he had drained himself, they got ready and she looked at him and told him, "look sweetie. I have loved you since we have been kids. I have always loved your kind and loving ways, but to be honest, I kind of like the new you." Preston burst out laughing, promising that he was going to keep the animal that she was enjoying. She told him not to play with her. They both laughed. It was time to get home and start their new and better life together. They wanted to share their lives with their families.

They got in the car, having just spent the most romantic night of their life, and in their minds, it was perfect. He drove Annabelle home and Mrs. Henderson spotted her daughter. She knew she had spent a wonderful night. Preston gave her a kiss and said, "I'll be back. We'll go out for dinner tonight." Annabelle came through the door, hugged her mother so hard that her mother knew this was the only thing that could make Annabelle happy. Thankfully, Preston came home. She knew Annabelle would be complete. Annabelle went upstairs, got ready for work but today was different. She felt complete, the boy she once knew was the man she wanted. Her body tingled all over that morning, replaying all the previous night's events. She had spent most of the afternoon and morning, fighting the affections of the wolf. She knew that her Preston had come back to her and was excited about the next chapter of their lives. An hour later, Preston got home. Preston's mother wondered how the evening had gone and Preston simply said "life could not be better." They spent the day together. Preston felt that after what he had put Annabelle through, she deserved a three-carat diamond ring. Preston knew it wasn't about the ring, he felt he owed it to Annabelle and nothing would stop him from giving this ring to her, to show how much he loved and adored her. What a wonderful night, they had had, after Annabelle saw him at babbling brook, the way she had looked at him was magical. He knew his life was complete, Annabelle back in his life, his brother always in his heart and his family behind him. He now saw the light. His mother shed a tear of delight and although the thought of Drew would always bring sorrow because he was not around to share their life, she knew his light would always shine bright in all their hearts and minds. Sometimes, in life, you need to feel the pain of sorrow and in Preston's case, his life was not complete without his brother at his side, but with Annabelle there, he knew it would all be okay.

CHAPTER 24

PRESTON HAD PLANNED TO PROPOSE to Annabelle the same night he purchased the ring. Lucky for him, it was the perfect size. He was going to take Annabelle, his parents and the Hendersons all out to dinner at Chez Marie. He had not shared his plans with Mr. or Mrs. Henderson or his father, that he was proposing tonight. He simply told them he was celebrating the rebirth of Preston and Annabelle. He had asked the Henderson's to show up at 8:30 pm and please, "don't be late." He was busy preparing the evening. He had ordered three dozen long stemmed red roses and a beautiful engagement cake that read "to the most beautiful and loving woman in my life." He had wanted to make it a special night after all the wasted years, but tonight was going to be special, and his mother was the only one that knew. He warned his mother not to smile and not give it away.

And of course, Mrs. Banks was going to try her best, but it was going to be difficult to hide her excitement. She had always known that the families would always come together. Preston had brought a new perspective to life and an new appreciation to all. Before they went out that night, Mr. Banks asked "why is there a twenty-five thousand dollar Amex charge to my account?", and she simply replied "you will see" and said "please, don't mention it again." Mr. Banks replied "ok dear." Preston had told his father to step on it, as he wanted to beat the Hendersons there. "I'm sure they'll be waiting, if we are late." Mrs. Banks gave her husband a stern look and said "step on it dear." When they arrived at Chez Marie, Preston jumped out of his father's car and simply went to the maître d'. He asked if the Hendersons had arrived and the maître d' replied, "not yet Mr. Banks." "We have set up the flowers, just the way you wanted." When they were seated, the elder Mr. Banks sat down at the table and was wondering what the big occasion was and then he ordered a Manhattan. Preston ordered whiskey sour, Mrs. Banks was not a big drinker, but tonight was a night to celebrate, and she order a Cosmopolitan. Mr. Banks looked at her puzzled as she wasn't a big drinker and she responded "yes dear it is a special night. Preston is home and Preston and Annabelle are back together. I, as a mother, could only be happier if Drew was here to share it." Mr. Banks sighed and then decided to go along with what they had planned because he was truly happy, as well.

As the drinks were served and Preston took his first sip, the Hendersons arrived. Mrs. Henderson noticed the flowers first and with a sly grin asked Preston "are those flowers for me?" He replied "no, but if Annabelle wants to share them with you that's her choice." Annabelle said "Are those flowers for me? Why so many?" Mr. Banks replied "why so many" I guess I paid for them" and laughed. Mrs. Banks shot him the dirtiest look and he knew he should zip it when Mrs. Banks punched him in the arm. Preston, at that moment, decided there was no reason to wait any longer. Suddenly out of the corner of Annabelle's eyes, a violinist started to play a beautiful melody. At that point, she realized that Preston had got down on one knee and simply said, "Annabelle, I have loved you from the first moment as a six-year-old boy and although it has been tough the last few years, I always knew I wanted you to be my wife." Annabelle replied "I will marry you, it's been my life's dream to marry you!" Preston opened the box that contained the three-carat diamond ring and Mr. Banks thought to himself, I know now where that charge came from.

They spent that night rejoicing, not only that Annabelle and Preston were about to be married, but the fact that the families would be joined through friendship and marriage. They could not be any happier. Mr. Banks knew he would be footing the bill but he didn't mind. He could not have been happier that he had his son back, he was very fond of his future daughter in-law. He was delighted that life, although bumpy, had found the right path, so he was happy to pay the bill and smiled at his family and future family.

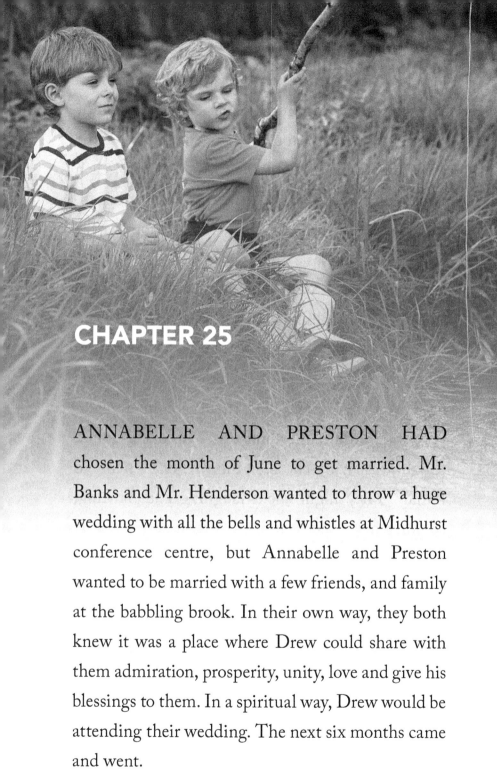

CHAPTER 25

ANNABELLE AND PRESTON HAD chosen the month of June to get married. Mr. Banks and Mr. Henderson wanted to throw a huge wedding with all the bells and whistles at Midhurst conference centre, but Annabelle and Preston wanted to be married with a few friends, and family at the babbling brook. In their own way, they both knew it was a place where Drew could share with them admiration, prosperity, unity, love and give his blessings to them. In a spiritual way, Drew would be attending their wedding. The next six months came and went.

The wedding day arrived, a sunny day with a slight breeze, with romantic music being played by the violinist. They stood on the river bank of the babbling brook and pronounced their love for each other, they were married where their love began. Mr. Henderson and Mr. Banks, were happy as the wedding was not as expensive as it could have been. It's amazing how life changes are made, good and bad, by simply taking a chance, and now they had their beautiful children and they had Halliburton to thank for it. Annabelle and Preston couldn't have been any happier with the reception, a quaint yet formal affair, the food was, without a doubt, delightful, having chosen a mixture of French and Italian. They night spent laughing and dancing, couldn't have been more perfect. They wouldn't have wanted their reception in any other place in the world. They felt like it was perfect, Preston had used a photo of his brother, bought a frame and in that way Drew was Preston's best man. The setting had been perfect, made more beautiful because the site was where true love had started for both Annabelle and Preston. The night of celebrating was finished.

The next day, they were ready to go on their honeymoon, going back to the first place they made love, Italy. They spent the most loving, romantic honeymoon they could ever have dreamed of. They had loved being in Italy before but now the wine, food and ambiance was even more wonderful. The romance, well let's just say, they needed to raise the air conditioning, if you get the point. Once the honeymoon was done, they were ready to settle into their beautiful home, located between Midhurst and Springwater in the town of Alcona. Preston understood, that if he was one day going to take over his father's business, he must work very hard. Annabelle woke up every day, knowing she had the love of her life by her side, and a dream job to go to. She felt so blessed and happy. No one knew she would be blessed yet again, she was three months pregnant.

The next six months were exciting, not only for the Banks, but also for the Hendersons and nine months to the day from their first night on the Amalfi coast, their son was born. Preston asked his father if he would mind if he named his grandson, Drew. Mr. Banks, his wife and the Hendersons, could not have been more proud of their children, and the fact that they named their baby after his late uncle. This had been so special. In their grandson's face, they could already see the similarities and feistiness and even the wry smile, that reminded them of Drew. They couldn't wait to share their combined love of young Drew, enjoy all that Preston, Drew and Anabelle had shared for many years. Drew had led the unity of his mother and father through their highs and their deepest lows. Now, the greatest joy with their grandson would be sharing the hills of Haliburton with their family into the next generation.

CHAPTER 26

IT HAD BEEN TWO YEARS SINCE LITTLE
Drew was born. The Banks and the Hendersons
were packing up, getting ready to spend the next two
glorious months showing their grandson how their
childhood had been filled with so many wonderful
memories and adventures and to teach little Drew,
where mommy and daddy's favorite place was, the
babbling brook. They sat around the table, as they
had done for so many years before, enjoying their
first meal as a family with the addition of young
Drew. Annabelle stood up and told everyone that
she was expecting twins, the mothers over the moon

with delight. The men, well they felt like Preston had played a big part. Annabelle passed young Drew to her mother and mother in-law. She grabbed her husband's hand. They took a walk to somewhere they had always gone, to get away, to enjoy their time together.

They knew that their brother would like to let them know he was there, with his approval of this new family news, that he would find his way to the babbling brook. As Preston helped his wife sit on the rock at the foot of the bubbling brook, he noticed a white butterfly land on his wife's belly. He felt a warm breeze and they both felt Drew's presence. I hope that in life we remember that we are never sure when we will lose a loved one and the impact it can have. It can rock the very ground that you walk in, so don't waste thinking that showing your love can wait. If there is someone you love share it, with them, as many times as you can.

I would like to dedicate this book in hopes that my children can experience the love that Drew and Preston had shared. The love of the outdoors and the many memories of a wonderful childhood waiting just over the horizon. As a parent, we can only wish the best for our children, although at times you may think that they are not watching, they are. You and your actions shape their lives. Don't assume that they know they are loved, show them. Any way you feel you could make their lives better, accommodate them. We have one life, don't waste it. Don't have regrets, have purpose. Love, unconditionally, as someone you love will see the light, and so will you. It's a wonderful life when it is filled with love, like the Banks and the Hendersons had.

Printed in the United States
By Bookmasters